MORE STORIES ABOUT SPACESHIPS AND CANCER

Casper Kelly

D1571842

FRIED SOCIETY
PRESS

"The Sensitive Person's Joke Book" originally appeared in *Necessary Fiction*.
Epilogue originally appeared as "Adventures in Stapling" in *MonkeyBicycle*.
"Sneezy" originally appeared in *The Cellar Door*.
"An Aspiring Haberdasher" is dedicated to Franz K. and the entertainment
industry.

Published by Fried Society Press

This is a work of fiction.

Printed in the United States of America
ISBN 978-0-9849407-0-7

Cover illustration by Kimiaki Yaegashi / Okimi.com
Fried Society Press logo by M. Brady Clark

First Printing, 2012

friedsociety.com

CONTENTS

For you

INTRODUCTION

You—yes, you!—are reading these words when something bursts out of the page causing bits of paper (or shards of plastic if you're using an e-reader) to explode outward. The skull is somehow bigger than the page it came out of and its eyes, lacking any surrounding skin, stare into yours with an unrelieved piercingness. Its skinless jaw, in an exaggerated grin, begins to move.

"I know what you're thinking!" it says. You drop the book/ebook to the floor and it bounces, once, and the skeleton moves out of it quickly and violently like being birthed from some multi-dimensional orifice, and smelling as such. It now towers above you.

"You're thinking, 'Do I really want to read this book?'" he says, this big skull with bits of skin hanging ... cheeks with pock marks, a goatee. A—is that?—yes, a beret. Tweed jacket with elbow patches, unbuttoned, no shirt only ribs showing through and bits of intestine. Blood stained khakis.

"With all the other stuff you could do—the TV shows to catch up on, the video games, the movies, and the learning how to cook, the hanging out with friends, the looking for your true love, or walking on the beach with your true love, the clipping your toenails, the needing to get on the old elliptical and all that. I get it.

"And even if you are going to read a *book*, why this one, from an unknown? With all those undisputed great books you need to check off! Chart toppers! Classics! Tolstoy, etc.! Or hip books in the cultural zeitgeist! That article about twenty hot writers under 30! I get it, buddy.

"You're thinking, even worse, *it's a short story collection*. A novel is like a developing relationship—" the "sh" in "ship" causes a bit of blood spittle to land on your nose, which he attempts to wipe off with a bony finger, smearing it—"a relationship that blossoms into love and, by the end, you feel like you've made and lost a friend.

"A short story collection, however, is like a hodgepodge of unsatisfying one night stands—none of them worthy of a real relationship i.e. carrying a novel. Short stories can be good, sure, it seems like they used to be good, like in the 1920s maybe, up through the 70s, when Hemingway and Fitzgerald wrote them, O'Connor and Cheever and Updike, and short stories were vital and talked about and studied and a part of the culture and could even be said to be *important*, and cool, but now they're not so cool and certainly not important, and they're more like modern poetry, i.e. they're made because that's what civilized societies are supposed to do but people don't really *care* about them anymore, people don't really read them, at least not hungrily like they once did, now it feels more like if they're read at all it's out of duty, like eating broccoli to get your vitamin A or whatever. Whatever vitamins broccoli provides. You barely get started with one and then you get hit with a gimmicky twist ending or worse, the ubiquitous small epiphany and/or ambiguous ending, like it ends with a description of a flock of birds against the sky in front of the sun and it says the sun is engulfing them, and you take from that phrasing of the sun engulfing the birds that the girl is going to get back into the car of her pleading abusive ex-boyfriend, she is the one really getting engulfed but not by the sun but by his abuse, although it doesn't literally say this, or even if she gets back in the car, but the violence of the engulfing line leads you to suspect it doesn't look good for this little lady making a change in her life, it seems like so many stories seem to work this way, it gets old doesn't it, it kind of sucks, but you're supposed to accept it sucks because it's 'subtle' or 'authentic' or 'luminous' and that's what real life is like and so forth but you know damn well in real life you damn well know if you get in the car with the abusive boyfriend or not, it's your life and it keeps going on.

And that's just the early stories, because make no mistake, all collections are frontloaded with the "good" stories, and one at the end, but the middle stories are a wasteland of dogs with fat ankles, pointless puff-pastries of words, fragments and/or "formal experiments," reading one is like having a one night stand with an embryo, just whatever shit they can shovel in the middle of the book so it's an acceptable, non-pamphlet/chapbook length. Oh, I understand your trepidation."

You decide the next time he starts talking you are going to run.

"But have no fear," he says. "I am here. Your host, Professor Badbones." He extends a boney hand which you clasp unconsciously, before you can even think to resist. The bones are wet and heavy but his grip is surprisingly gentle. "If terrible horror movies can enjoy a new life on TV thanks to a gimmicky horror host, why not short stories? Let's give it a chance, shall we? Also, allow me to introduce you to my cohost. Snervely, get out here."

Off in the corner there is a small creature, apparently made out of lip skin and patches of hair. It hisses out of its toothless hole.

You run.

Rounding the corner you turn back to see if they're gaining. But they're nowhere in sight.

Then, a voice.

"We're in your head now!" says Professor Badbones. He laughs again, and it's almost like you can feel the phlegm from his laughter splashing inside your head. "We're in your brain, rummaging through your most secret thoughts. I am grinding my hips against one of your high school memories right now.

You may find it affects your sensory perception."

Your eyes pulse a sliding blurriness. You feel a twinge inside your head and hear a grunt. You fall.

"Hey, ever feel life is one cruel joke? Well, the characters in our first story are about to discover just that … hee hee hee!"

And as you try to get up, your vision blurs again and you start to hallucinate. About a bar. And maybe a duck ….

THE SENSITIVE PERSON'S JOKE BOOK

A man and a duck walk into a bar.
The bartender says, "I'm sorry. We don't serve gorillas."
"This isn't a gorilla, he's a duck," says the man.
The bartender replies, "I was talking to the duck."

The man and duck sit quietly for a moment. Somewhere in the distance pool balls collide.

Finally, the man opens his mouth. He speaks calmly and carefully to the bartender. "Yes, it is true I have a disproportionately small forehead and thick nose. I am large and, in spite of careful grooming, hirsute. I have been made well aware of these things—in middle school particularly. Despite these traits I could in no way be mistaken for a gorilla, not in good faith, and I apologize if I'm wrong, but I suspect your error was intentional, for cruel and comic effect. Sir, we did not ask to be in your joke. We didn't wake up this morning saying we would like to be someone's punch line. We came to this place, a place of business, expecting goods and services rendered with professionalism."

The duck's eyes flit around taking in everything except the eyes of his friend or the bartender. "Quack," he says.

The man continues, "If you must know, I just lost my job and my friend's wife of seventeen years left him a year ago today.

We are here to commiserate and more importantly we are here to drink. Now, if you would, please get us a pitcher of Pabst Blue Ribbon. As I said, I have just lost my job and so am on a tight budget."

If the bartender has a reaction he doesn't show it. He leaves to get a pitcher.

The man's eyes dart over to two women at the other end of the bar. They are moderately attractive and dressed in a way that turns up the volume of that moderateness to be quite loud. The man's eyes seem to tell the duck they should make an approach, that the way to get over a divorce is to get back in the fray. And this they do. Later, the duck insists on picking up the tab but is unsuccessful because the loss to the man's pride at not paying his half is greater than any money saved.

In the unfair way life works, it is not the duck but the man who goes home with a woman that night. This hurts the duck. It only serves to reinforce his feelings of loneliness/isolation/unattractiveness. The duck feels he deserves the hook-up more than the man. He had talked to her first, the woman with the pretty brown eyes—Vanessa—and had been nicer and expressed more interest in her thoughts and feelings. He does not have bad breath. Nor does he look like a gorilla.

No, that's petty. That's petty. It's just that today is the year anniversary of his divorce, a divorce his wife had initiated through no fault of his own. One loveless, lonely year—while his friend had had more than a few girlfriends that he rotated effortlessly and seemingly without care. If God was a parent and we the kids, thought the duck, and love were pizza from a pizza restaurant that one is taken to after, say, a soccer game or perhaps lessons in Kung Fu, the God/parent would have surely seen the duck's empty plate and generously proffered him a warm gooey slice of pepperoni. Surely he wouldn't just give the entire pizza to someone else and give none to the duck.

"I'm sorry to leave you in the lurch, buddy," his friend had said, "but look at her, she's built like a brick shithouse." But the duck thought she was built nothing like a brick shithouse. Nothing at all. She smelled nice. She looked soft. Also she wasn't red with white lines where the cement is.

The duck flies home, both happy for and envious of his friend. There should be a word for that, he thinks. *Henvious.* The duck dated a hen once. She was a bossy thing, owing perhaps to being an only child. His friends couldn't stand her but he adored her. Maybe on some level he likes being bossed around. Being told what to do. Maybe that's why things fell apart with his wife. They both wanted to be told what to do.

"Henvious." It's a good word. Maybe he could write a book of such words. Like Sniglets. Then again, there's probably already a word for it. Probably French.

2.

The man goes home with the woman, Vanessa.

"My vagina is so big," she says, "I'll give you one hundred dollars if you have anything it can't take."

The man puts in a shoe and it is sucked right in. Then he puts in a flashlight and that too is sucked in. Finally he puts his face down there to get a better look and he is sucked in, too.

The man wanders around in the dark until he hears a noise.

"Is someone else in here?" asks the man.

"Yeah, I've been here for years," a voice says.

"Help me find my flashlight and we can get out of here," says the man.

"Hell," says the other man, "help me find my keys and we can drive out!"

They feel around for a while and come upon on a small fleshy outcropping. They sit in the dark.

"I'm surprised I didn't notice Vanessa's hips were wide enough to contain an actual car," says the man, who, as has been mentioned, has more than a passing resemblance to a gorilla.

7

"One might say it strains credulity."

"You met her at a bar, didn't you?" asks the second man, whose hair and beard are overgrown, and wears a worn cowboy hat and threadbare, moldy clothes at least ten years out of fashion. "I thought I could hear music. Muffled and far away. I miss it. The outside world. The people."

"And yet, we are inside a person."

"Yes," agrees the second man. He licks his dry lips and spits.

The first man continues: "There's something here. Of why there's this void between people. Why we're near and yet not. Why this emotional distance. Between men and women. Between all people."

The second man doesn't saying for a while. The air is thick and humid. Then the second man speaks. "You talk like a pussy," he says. He grunts as he stands wearily up, brushes off his jeans. "Maybe you belong here."

The man listens to the second man walk off in the darkness and doesn't say anything. He doesn't get to ask his questions, like "How did you survive here?" and "What did you eat?"

The man lies down on his back and tries to appreciate it. The miracle of it. Take it in so he can remember. The muskiness. The earthiness. This human being, this Vanessa, who has big brown eyes that seem to have a squint of merriment about something she wasn't telling you yet.

The man winces at the memory of putting a flashlight in her, a shoe. Why would he do such a thing? Because she had asked. It was expected of him. And now here he was. In a vagina that from the outside was normal, but from the inside perhaps infinite. A miracle of space and time, something with alternate dimensions, perhaps. Quantum something. Or magic. If science could harness this, he thought, just think of that. He scratched his wide nose. Crowded tenement apartments could be mansions on the inside. One airplane could carry thousands of people in comfort. It would save fuel. You could put all the world's pollution in a tiny box and shoot it off to space ...

The man awakens to the sound of a car revving and lights in his face. He pretends he is still asleep and does not ask for a ride.

3.

An American, an Englishman, and a Polack are due to face a firing squad.

The American is first to be lined up against the wall. As the soldiers raise their rifles and take aim, he shouts, "Avalanche!" The soldiers turn around to look and by the time they realize it is a hoax, the American has made his escape.

Next the Englishman lines up against the wall. Just as the soldiers raise their rifles he shouts, "Flood!" Again, they turn around to see what the problem is and so the Englishman runs to safety.

Finally, the Polack lines up against the wall. He is greatly impressed by his cunning colleagues and is determined to come up with a similar diversion.

So as the soldiers raise rifles and aim, he shouts, "Fire!"

On the ground, bleeding, bleeding and full of bullets, the Polack speaks haltingly, a whisper, barely audible, audible to no one but himself, through the sound of blood spurting and sucking air. "Poland has … cough … Poland has long been ass-raped by history. We fought our way out of the frying pan of the Nazis only to fall into the fire of Stalin's Russia. And yet we persist. And what do we get for this indomitable human spirit?" Before he can answer—although presumably the question was rhetorical—he dies. He dies alone, with no one seeing him. Or so he thought. Above, from a window on the top floor of the villa where the army has made its headquarters, the duck watches.

The duck is filled with sickening anxiety. He's really gonna be thrown in the buzz saw for this one. The colonel is going to chew him up and spit him out for this. Two escapees. An American. And an Englishman! The duck tries to justify himself in imaginary conversation with the colonel. Yes, I am in charge of these men. But I didn't hire them. It is not my fault they are so stupid.

The duck waddles down the steps to the yard and paces in front of the men. His anxiety flares up into fury. He quacks until he is hoarse. How, yet again, could they have allowed the prisoners to escape? He has said repeatedly to tie the prisoners to the post. Tie them securely. Also, lock the door. Always lock the door. Also, have one designated person to look behind if someone says "Flood!" or "Tornado!" so that the majority can maintain visual contact with the prisoner. Also, just exercise common sense. If someone yells "Avalanche!" think—do we live near a mountain? Wouldn't one hear an avalanche, wouldn't one be so loud one could barely hear someone screaming "Avalanche?" Consider the person yelling it, and what their motivations might be. When a prisoner yells "Topless Carwash!" or "Flying Saucer!" or "Look, there's a second firing squad behind you, aiming at you!" consider that they may be lying.

The men bring up the Polack, who they did successfully shoot. The duck dismisses their entreaties with a wave of his wing. Do not bring up to me the Polack. It was only through dumb luck that you got the Polack. That is nothing to be proud of. And also, the preferred term is "Pole." Polack is an ethnic slur.

The duck waddles to the break room for a coffee and purchases, from the snack machine, a Mrs. Freshlee branded snack of refined flour and corn syrup, which he consumes thoughtlessly and joylessly in his office, rotating it and breaking off tiny bites in his beak. The fiery loathing crumples into self-loathing, much like the Polack crumpled when he was shot. What did the American, the Englishmen, the Pole ever do that they deserved to be brought in front of a firing squad? It would have to be a good reason, right? But if it's a good reason, why wouldn't the colonel tell him?

The duck wonders again how he, the duck, came to be in charge of a firing squad anyway. He had set out to be a pharmacist. He had gotten into a school and had bought the textbooks. He liked the idea of giving people medicine. But then he was dissuaded by the thought of having to ring up peoples' other purchases—batteries, condoms, clocks, toy floaties, diet bars, lotion. The duck had never enjoyed working retail. So instead of following his true dream, he somehow ended up here. It's a steady gig, pays pretty well, he thinks. He has a house that maintains comfortable temperatures with insulation in accordance with the latest Energy Star rating.

The duck thinks, I went from giving out medicine to giving out death. I had bought the textbooks—I had them. Still, the duck dips the piece of glazed cake into the coffee rapidly, and swallows, I don't shoot the people. It's not like I pull the trigger. But the little voice inside the duck knows that when you tell the soldiers to shoot, you are responsible, it is the same as shooting. *You're a shooter.*

The duck goes back to the break room for a second dance with Mrs. Freshlee. The first bite of her is not pleasing at all. Neither is the next one. And he follows that not-pleasantness until the cake is gone. He feels horror that a man died today. He feels horror that two men escaped on his watch. He feels horror at both his success and his failure. There should be a word for that. *Fuccess. Sailure.* The fear of it. He can't win and he can't leave. He's stuck for sure. Heading for the colonel's buzz saw. *Shooter.*

In the yard the soldiers cut up, smoke, wait the fifteen minutes until the next prisoner is brought out. The duck approaches them, casually twirling a blindfold around his wing. The men snap to attention. One of them, Felder, oblivious, still waddles around quacking angrily in some sort of imitation of the duck. When he does notice the duck, he clumsily brings his hand to a full salute next to his shame-reddened face.

The duck wishes there was some distraction he could yell to make his own escape. Ice Cream Truck. Armageddon.

The duck puts on the blindfold. He thinks of his ex-wife.

She didn't stop loving him. He just stopped being the him that she loved.

"Fire," he says.

4.

A rabbi, a priest, a lawyer, a blonde, a duck, and a man who bears more than a casual resemblance to a gorilla have all died and gone to heaven where they meet St. Peter at the Pearly Gates.

"Well," says St. Peter. "It's very crowded in heaven right now so we have to be more selective about who gets in. I have here a tape measure and several pitchers of water. Whoever can pee the farthest distance gets into heaven. The rest of you will burn in hell."

As angels pour cups of water, the man sidles up behind the duck, his eyes twinkling. "What's a duck like you doing in a nice joint like this?"

The duck turns to see his friend and is happy. There is a patting of shoulders, a hand shake, falling into a sort of one-arm-one-wing hug.

"Workplace accident," says the duck. The man tells a funny story about a woman, her vagina, a flashlight, and getting run over by a car.

The duck sounds like he is laughing and then sounds like he's choking. Then the man realizes the duck is crying.

"What's wrong, friend?" asks the man.

"I guess I had hoped in death I could let my guard down. That there would be someone in charge, someone who would use that power to be kind and good. Instead, we continue to face these arbitrary indignities. Why is pee distance any sort of criteria for one's eternity? There is no end to this. No end. And how can I be expected to pee any distance at all? I'm a duck. A duck."

The man puts his hand on the duck's ruffled feathers. "Hey," he says. "I will probably pee a short distance as well. You know with my prostate. We will go to hell together. Besides," says the man, "the blonde is sure to go with us. And she's kind of cute."

But the duck doesn't want to go to hell. Or to a desert island. Or a bar. Or a church. Or a farmer's barn. Or anywhere else.

"Just stop," says the man. "Stop talking. Look here. Look."

And while the rabbi pees in a manner that shows he is stingy, and the priest pees in a way entailing attraction to young boys, and the lawyer pees in a fashion showing that his character is less than upright, and the blonde pees in a manner both sexual and remarkably stupid, the duck and the man go off to a corner and take just a moment to enjoy the pearliness of the outside of the gate, and the blue sky that goes on forever, and the cloud they're on, standing on it, its softness, the softness of standing on a cloud, until their names are called.

INTERMISSION

"Well, that ending was a real pisser, hee hee hee!" Professor Badbones says. The laugh feels scripted, forced, and the more he draws it out the more you can't help feeling a bit sorry for him.

Professor Badbones holds up a pipe.

"Mind if I smoke?"

He sits in a leather smoking chair. Behind him, bookshelves, like a study, but not. The walls are reddish-pink meat. You presume that would be your brains.

He takes a drag on his pipe, then another, and lets out a leisurely puff of smoke although most of it leaks out of his chest cavity. "Kind of gives a new definition to smoking jacket. Well, at least I don't have to worry about lung cancer! Hee hee!"

"I guess it's fitting that story number one was about 'number one'. Let's hope story number two doesn't follow that trend, ha ha ha! But at our current rate it will, in terms of quality! Hee hee! Right, Snervely?"

Badbones waves his hand and your eye is directed to a restaurant by a park where the people are...

TAKING A SHIT IN THE FUTURE

Mixtopia - (noun)
1. A mix between a utopia and a dystopia where some things are unbelievably better while simultaneously other things are hellishly worse, e.g. "The warm slappable realness of this sexbot's thighs almost distracts me from the painful sickness I have from this radioactive corn. That's living in a mixtopia for ya!"
2. A frozen yogurt chain in Southern California that was known for its numerous toppings (both of the chocolate and fresh fruit variety) that could be mixed into one's frozen yogurt. Declared bankruptcy during the radioactive corn uprisings of 2112.

We were having brunch, my wife, my sister, some of her friends, their kids, over at that new place by the park that does the Thai/Southern fusion, *Thai Y'all*—peanut sauce grits, Massaman gravy biscuits and the like. Good stuff. A little heavy. But the weather was nice, not too hot, and the coffee good.

My sister has cool friends. We're all laughing and joking and there's a good rhythm to the conversation. There was a good balance between people talking about themselves and asking thoughtful questions of others; nobody was too domineering of the conversation, and there was a good span of topics because one woman's a doctor, one owns a restaurant in a sketchy part of town and she packs a pistol to ward off robberies, one's a grad student from Spain, and so on. A good thing to sort of pull me out of my Sunday morning "What am I doing with my life?" doldrums.

After we had paid and were just sitting there drinking coffee and holding on to the pleasantness of the brunch, one of the people there, Madison, who had her dog with her, excused herself to take the dog for a walk.

I said I imagined he'd need a potty break what with all those leftovers the kids had been feeding him.

And Madison said, "Oh no. He doesn't go to the bathroom anymore. He's completely fixed."

I asked her what she meant by that and said my understanding of "fixed" referred to some different bodily functions.

And Madison, excited she'd found someone who hadn't heard about this yet, told me about this new procedure they can do where you don't have to go to the bathroom anymore.

"What do you mean? This dog doesn't shit or pee? Ever?" I asked. I winced realizing I'd just said "shit" in front of the kids but luckily they were over on the other side of the table and not really paying attention.

"Yes." She nodded, beaming. That's exactly what she meant.

Most of the table had heard of this, including my wife, and she was a little surprised I hadn't.

That's impossible, I said. It's the laws of conservation of matter and energy. Thermodynamics. Food goes in the body. That matter has to go somewhere.

And Mark said no, it's some new procedure. Apparently it converts all waste into waves or something.

"Radio waves? Radioactive waves? Light waves? Ocean waves?" I asked.

"I don't know. Some kind of invisible waves. They're harmless."

"I can't believe you haven't heard of this. You always hear about these things before me," said my wife.

I shook my head at all this. It was true that after being

information overloaded I had laid off the data stream for a bit. But I was still skeptical. I thought they were putting me on. I took out my phone and started reading about it. Yeah. It was real. It was first developed in Japan. It converted matter into energy which it somehow dispersed harmlessly, without releasing too much heat. Patented technology. And it had recently been approved for pets in America.

"Cloony is much more comfortable this way," said Madison. "He never has to worry or wait until I get home to go. Now when we walk it's just to walk."

"But how does he mark his territory?" I asked.

"He still tries. But nothing comes out. He's trying less and less now." She shrugged. "I think he's much happier now."

"It's going to get approved for people," said Mark. "It already is in Asia. Rich people are doing it. Movie stars. The government provides the procedure to incontinent people in nursing homes. They're doing it with Alzheimer's patients, people who can't take care of themselves. People in comas. Think of that—somebody has to clean all that shit from people in comas. It's ultimately going to be a huge cost savings and all that."

"Asia is always ahead of us on these things," added Taylor.

"I heard the big market is going to be with babies. Parents are going to love not having to deal with babies pooping constantly. And potty training," Mark said.

"Really? They're going to do this to little babies? After all this effort with natural food and natural childbirth and all that? That seems weird," said my wife.

"Just you wait. It seems weird now ..." Mark said. "It's coming. Diaper companies are already freaking out. Having emergency strategy meetings."

"I wish I could get it done retroactively," said Taylor, patting his stomach. "I don't think coconut milk and chiles go with French toast. I'm just saying."

A few years passed, maybe seven. And sure enough the

procedure spread out. It was just like how it must have been with braces, with LASIK, cars, cell phones, boob jobs, fire, houses, refrigerators, etc. At first it seemed frivolous, and then it kind of became really good to have, and then it became necessary. Public places started offering fewer bathrooms. There were stories of college kids renting apartments without any toilets at all. Excusing yourself to go to the bathroom became a signifier that you were old-fashioned, out of touch, or, worse, too poor to afford the procedure. The poor still shit. They would always shit.

My wife had it done. My kids had it done. My parents. And then when my office removed the bathrooms on my floor (sighting the high price of water) and I had to go downstairs to the central lobby just to pee (which I did a lot because I had the world's tiniest bladder and I drank massive amounts of coffee to force myself to be excited and enthusiastic about work duties, which in my heart of hearts I found pointless and soul crushing. What do I do for a living? Does it matter? I help make content I find uninteresting to sell things I find pointless to people I find baffling). I had to walk downstairs to pee and it felt like everyone knew what I was doing, it was almost a walk of shame, all the young bucks watching me pass by from their conference rooms where they had initiative meetings, the young Turks gunning for my position because I was getting old, out of touch with the kids and all the new shit, not e-gloving and bandana planking and all that other shit. I entertained the idea that if I could be one of the last holdouts, it would become cool to pee and shit, something really novel and retro, but in truth it just made me feel old, but not too old because the old were doing it in droves, too. It just made me feel like a misfit. Someone who was no longer participating in the culture, no longer accepting the new. Someone who was no longer valuable for the company, or maybe the world at large.

So I got a consultation. It was surprising how cheap it had gotten. I had been wrong about the poor always shitting, I guessed. There was a glut of out-patient offices in strip malls competing for a dwindling number of people who hadn't already done it. And I signed up. Signed the forms.

That next week I returned to the office. Have you had anything to eat or drink in the past twelve hours? No. Did you take the enema? Yes. And do you have any allergies? Et cetera. My doctor was very young and pretty and even in her outfit that revealed nothing you could just tell everything under there was real nice. I thought about how she had to put stuff up people's asses all day, but I guess they paid her enough so she had the money to help her forget it.

I put on the gown and had a sudden pang. Yesterday when I was taking my last shit I didn't really stop to think "This is going to be my last shit," and I guess I should have. I should have taken care to try to remember it.

I did pee one last time before they put me under. They asked me to clear my bladder, so I was peeing one last time in this small outpatient doctor's office bathroom, with its plastic dispos-all box for medical waste mounted on the wall, and a yellowing poster about prostate health, dribbling into the toilet because I don't have to pee that much, it wasn't a powerful one, and I was thinking I should have peed my name in the snow one last time maybe, not that it snows near me, or that I've ever done it, or peed on my wife's face, a "golden shower," not because I wanted to but just because I won't be able to do it now, ever, but then I was finished and I flushed it away and then I was on the table and they put the gas mask on me and the pretty doctor got fuzzy, fuzzier, totally a smear of color, like my vision when I would take my glasses off, before I got my new eyes, just everything sort of vague and pillowy, comforting really …

"You may experience some residual urination or defecation but that should clear up in the next several days," the doctor said, and handed a pamphlet to my wife.

"So everything went okay?"

"Went great!"

"Do I need to wait before I eat anything?"

"Nope. You can go eat whatever you want! You're all set! You're good to go!"

"So, I can—I'm okay to leave?"

"Yep. Just go left on the hallway and follow the signs to check out."

I felt like I should have had more questions. But the pretty doctor was hitting me hard with the I-am-done-with-you-and-your-questions-I-hear-every-time-and-I'm-ready-for-the-next-patient-so-I-can-make-money-faster body language.

As I got dressed, I touched the bandage on my stomach. She said the incision was about the size of my finger tip. I pressed it and it didn't even feel sore.

On the way home my wife and I stopped for hamburgers and milkshakes. Lots of mayo. Fries. Onion rings. Onion rings dipped in ranch, honey mustard. When they did the procedure, when they put in that atomizer or whatever it was, they set it so only 80% of the calories would hit my system. It was atomizing 20% of the food before it could even be digested. It was a standard thing in America and they could adjust the percentage based on my results. I'd never been really overweight so it was not a huge issue, but it wouldn't hurt to lose a few. It was nice to not have to watch my eating. I could now eat things just because it was fun. I guess this was another reason the procedure was so popular. My wife asked if I was kicking myself for not doing this sooner.

I realized you didn't see a lot of fat people anymore. Not in real life. There were still fat people in videos and video games. Funny fat people like Johnny Lard or the Old Biddies. My wife said they got the procedure too, but they just set it to put extra calories into their system, instead of less. I thought it seemed easier to use computer graphics to add pounds for the videos but she said no, when they appeared at awards shows and on red carpets they were still fat. I took her word for it.

At the office I drank coffee and, without the full bladder signaling I needed a break, would work for longer stretches until other, different, signals came up: my left leg falling asleep, a gradual inability to focus, a sudden realization I was staring into space. I got up to stretch my legs. I took more regular trips to the candy dish in Conference B. I almost wanted to take up smoking, which I guess I could since it no longer caused cancer.

Going to lunch I passed the bathroom and I fought the temptation—the habit?—to go in. I don't know why. To just pull out my dick for a moment of intimate nudity in the middle of the day? A quick spread of the ass cheeks on the porcelain for old times' sakes, a bit of hairy animal rawness tucked away from the outer office beige banality? A place to grunt instead of discuss P13 reports? Some brief escape? Was it the cozy privacy of a bathroom stall, an office with a door available to all as needed, and not just to the senior execs?

My stomach vibrated after meals. Not like a stomach growling but more like the inside flutter when you're at a concert next to speakers that are very very loud. It was subtle, infrequent, almost not noticeable, like a slight ringing in the ears. It almost had a rhythm, but not quite.

I asked about this in my follow up.

"Yes," said the doctor, a different one, the pretty doctor was probably on a beach somewhere trying to forget about assholes. "The vibros are perfectly normal. Most people find they die down over time. Or they just get used to them and stop noticing. You'll be fine."

"It's been a few months."

"You'll be fine. Just live your life and you'll soon forget they're there."

"What if I want a reversal?"

"A reverse what?"

"Reverse the procedure."

The doctor laughed. "That would be pretty hard because you have no intestines. We had to take out your intestines to fit in the atomizer. Don't over think this. You're fine. Enjoy yourself!"

He stood up and I stood up with him, unthinkingly. He had his hands in his pockets and swiveled to half face to door.

"If you have any questions, don't hesitate to call my office."

"But, I have a question."

He stared at me impatiently, his mouth in a wincing smile.

I forgot what I was going to ask.

He patted my shoulder and was gone.

Outside my favorite bar I saw a lineup of bathroom stall walls leaning sadly by the dumpster. I ran my hands along the silver toilet paper holder and the graffiti carved in with knives or sharpied. Phone numbers. Lewd drawings. Bumper sticker philosophy and corrections and additions to said philosophy. Bathroom walls, I thought, were the original anonymous message boards.

"We'll still have a room with a sink and a mirror. Women will still need to freshen up," said the owner, "and we'll keep one toilet in each for vomiting, and hookups, and what have you. But we're taking most of that wasted space back to add another booth, another game machine, and a bit more storage for all these new hallucination beers. People get real particular about which kind they want and if you don't keep a big enough selection they'll go somewhere else. They have one where you hallucinate just animated butterflies. One each, at least one each, for all the sports teams. And they're always adding ones with new supermodels. A year ago they had no such thing as designer hallucination beer and now they have too many."

I had always loved pissing at bars. You're flirting with a girl. You've got to pee. You lope to the bathroom. The music is vibrating through you, you feel at peace, you feel happy, the walls are swaying almost poetically from your inebriated unbalance. You take out your dick. Hello old friend. I wonder if she will meet you tonight. A pause in the action. Noting how the color palette of the piss—is it watered down lemonade or the color almost of orange juice concentrate? Maybe there's a cigarette butt or sanitizer to aim at and try to demolish like some first person shooter. The nods, eye contacts, or lack of eye contacts with the other men. Washing your hands. The cathartic rediscovery of yourself as you look up from your wet hands to your face in the mirror. Yes, this is me. This my life. This is me happy. Remember this.

Another memory. Peeing in the shower. A clump of hair is clogging the drain. Pulled it back with my big toe and pee. Peeing without having to hold my penis always felt freeing.

Friday night. The kids were upstairs fighting 3-D battles of simulated island survival and the grownups were downstairs playing CULTURE WHORE. It was my wife and I, the Gibbons, the Costellos, and the Hartins. We were the second bottle of Malbec into a conversation about a series of popular Musical Nudist Westerns based on a reimagining of that High School police procedural video game that was big ten years ago. They were ribbing me about not liking these movies and saying I'm a bit of a snob about it. Maybe I was. I just wanted to get away for a minute. I got up and said I had to go to the bathroom.

There was a pause as if I was making a joke. And then people burst out laughing because I had been caught in a lie.

I tried to pretend I was kidding and really just wanted to get some more chips from the kitchen but no one believed me.

That said, I always liked the Gibbons, the Costellos, and the Hartins (not so much the Hartins), and we never seemed to have them over enough.

Another memory: the pleasurable feeling of having to shit terribly and hunting for a good book in a race against time. It's not often in life one has to race against time. Maybe back when there were movie theaters having to race to get to the movie on time. I barely remember that.

Or that satisfaction of getting out a really huge shit, pushing out that really painful stubborn fucker, trying to relax and then push, relax, push, and wondering how bad is it going to get, are you going to be able to take it or is it going to split you open, and wondering if this is at all like childbirth, or not at all, and afterwards feeling like you've really done something. Walking out of the bathroom light on your heels, feeling thirty pounds lighter. The pleasure from pleasure is great, obviously. But the pleasure of being in pain, and then having that pain taken away, is almost better, because it makes you happy although you are just back to where you were.

Would "shit" and "stinks like shit" and "built like a brick shithouse" and "knock the buzzard off a shit wagon" become odd phrases that linger on past their original meaning, like "keep your powder dry," "spitting image," or "hang up the phone?"

One night I couldn't sleep. My stomach was vibrating with an irregularity that made it hard to tune out. The old atomizer was working on a pretty irregular dinner I guessed, some leftover steak, some lo mein, a sweet potato, ice cream. All of it being sent out to the universe in waves.

I remembered we had an old radio in the attic. It was my

great-grandfather's. We kept it because it looked cool. So big and strange. For a while we had it on the coffee table as a conversation piece.

I got out of bed, quietly shut the bedroom door, and crept up into the attic. There it was, next to some clothes and old computers. It had all those weird curves and swoops and old timey LED lights and a folding handle up top. And an antennae! I forgot about those.

In the dining room, I plugged it in and was surprised it still worked. The next thing I didn't want my family to see. I put the antennae to my gut and started pushing the buttons that tuned up and down the radio spectrum. Past the Ukrainian station. The Gospel one. Surprised they still had stations at all. Until I came to an area, around 96FM on the dial, where I heard packets of noise and silence that seemed to match those in my stomach, or rather where my stomach used to be. I slowed down and adjusted the buttons more finely.

BLMMMMMM. BLLMMMMMMMM.

I lied down on the floor with the radio on my belly. Bending the antennae around it. I discovered a knob for even finer tuning and I twisted it slowly.

YOUUUU. YOUUUUUUUUUUUULL, said the radio.

The voice sounded almost British, but also like me. My hair stood on end and I become aware of my heart beating faster, sweating. My stomach vibrated again.

HELP. HELP. Chirpkk. (Or was it "Health?")

124 ALMONNNNNNnnnnnnnnnnnssskkkkkk

124 ALMOND.

That's what it sounded like.

I lay there another twenty minutes but that was the last of it.

Help? Eat 124 almonds?

That morning after the kids went to school I told my wife about it. She said I was reading into things. Like how people would find shapes in clouds or messages in backwards audio. She thought tuning a radio into a stomach atomizer was a good idea though. Maybe something I could work into a funny video. She said I could make a song out of it. Maybe something would catch on and go viral. I knew she was right about it meaning nothing. It was nothing, just random sounds I turned into words. But I couldn't help wanting to believe it. I couldn't help it. Maybe it was the fact that it was coming out of me, a place so deep inside of me. It was a message coming out of me. And we want things to have meaning. We crave a special meaning just for us.

I searched 124 Almond and didn't come up with much. One thing that did come up was 124 Elmond. It was an address in town. Two, actually. 124 Elmond Drive and 124 Elmond Court.

At work I took an early lunch break to check it out. 124 Elmond Court was a house in a run-down part of town. I knocked and an older woman answered, maybe 115. I explained to her about the radio messages from my stomach. She nodded and said, "You got the message. Yes." My heart jumped. She looked around nervously and said, "Come in. Come in and meet the others of our group."

When I entered her house she didn't stand aside to let me pass and I had too brush awkwardly against her. I stood in her foyer, looking at old movie posters and a box of plates.

"I'm sorry," she said. "I thought you knew I was kidding. Bad joke. I wasn't serious."

"Has anyone else come here, getting the same message?" I asked.

"No," she said, laughing. "I just thought maybe this was one of those prank shows. Where you get a prize. I was playing along. I don't know. I just thought it would be funny if there were a group here. Like a plot twist in a horror movie or something," she said.

She did say once due to a glitch in GPS directions people would drive by her house expecting an office supply store. But that was thirty years ago.

I peeked into the living room, maybe expecting a group seated on the floor, or a half circle of folding chairs. Instead it was just boxes. On her kitchen table was a pile of cutlery.

"Well, I better get back to packing," she said. "I'm moving."

124 Elmond Drive was just a few blocks away, an empty lot that used to be a gas station between a Persian bagel shop and a used furniture place.

I bought a bagel and ate it parked in my car. Then I took out my radio to see what I could pick up. I heard occasional noises, sort of metallic. I sort of made out the word "handle" or "hammer" in an Arabic accent but it was a stretch.

On the lamp post near my car a flyer caught my eye. The Shitting Museum, it said. Opening night was this Friday.

My wife and I and the Gibbons arrived at a signless warehouse with a line of well-to-do art patron looking people out front. The Shitting Museum was not a museum but an art performance. Out front we paid our money and an art student with black bangs handed us each a bag and motioned us inside to a large hallway. It was lined with a bunch of different bathroom doors recycled from various places. Most said Men or Women in a variety of fonts. Some used pictures. One, probably from an old fish restaurant, had the words BUOYS and GULLS written in cursive rope within life preservers. Another had pictures of dogs and says POINTERS and SETTERS. Not sure what that would be from, a pet store? DICKS and JANES. A picture of a cow and a bull. A hand holding up a finger and another forming a hole. An eel and a clam.

I opened one of the men's doors and went inside. Against the wall were urinals, stalls, all different kinds. The artist must have picked them up cheap from thrift stores and dumpsters all over. Some of the stalls were sleek and modern like from offices, some older, yellowed, dirty. I found one of the larger stalls, a handicapped one, and closed the door. Inside the bag were the instructions and the little tube/bag/enema thing, which I inserted in my ass. The instructions said I needed to sit and wait for ten minutes.

In the stall was a screen. On the screen was a video of various animals taking a shit. A dog crouched in a flower garden. I read the artist's bio that was included in the directions. Apparently she never got the procedure and now she's being hailed as a genius. Her work is generating a lot of heat. Her statement of artistic intent talks about staying in touch with our animal selves and all that. All that stuff I sort of thought about before I decided to do the procedure anyway.

About eight minutes in there was a weird feeling in my ass and it started foaming. Expanding. I peered around and saw brown foam oozing out. I guess this was the "shitting." The simulated dump people were talking about. But it was like foam, not like shit, or diarrhea, and there's no feeling of your bowels being emptied. It was more like what you would get if you shook up a warm Coke and sprayed it in your ass. It not only didn't really evoke memories of shits past, it dimmed those old memories with this new false sensation. This shit was too foamy. That was my opinion. But maybe the people who had this procedure done at birth would appreciate it. The bathroom smells were pretty accurate. I read that the artist used her own waste to help achieve that effect.

When the foaming stopped I wiped and washed and met up with my wife and the Gibbons and we went into the big room. The artist was shitting on stage. Smearing it on the wall. We all agreed that must take some skill to do on schedule like that. For a moment it seemed like she was going to throw some at the audience, but she stopped short. Maybe a lawsuit thing. She smeared some more on the walls. On her face. Did she eat some of her own shit? Yes. That was the climax. And then the lights come up and it was time to go.

My wife and I and the Gibbons walked back to our cars. We didn't really feel like eating, but decided to go for a drink. We all agreed the show was interesting. I held on to that pamphlet of instructions as a souvenir. They're in a drawer somewhere.

I don't remember the last time my stomach vibrated. I'm not sure if it did stop or if I just can't notice it anymore. Eventually the radio ended up back in the attic. Or maybe the trash, I'm not sure.

This morning I took a shower. I used to pee in the shower. The pressure from having to pee used to cause me to wake up with a hard-on. Or maybe it was just erotic dreams that gave me hard-ons. Of course I had already had the dick procedure and so I was hard when I wanted to be, so I made myself hard when I woke up in the morning, because I liked it. Also, I sang in the shower a lot more since I got that thing that automatically tuned my voice when I sang. They put it in my larynx. Although it didn't completely feel like my voice coming out of me I could still sing awesomely well in the shower, or at karaoke, or anywhere else. Right on key. So there was that.

INTERMISSION

"Well, I hope you just didn't flush away ten minutes of your life with that story. Ha ha ha!" he says. "Eh, Snervely?"

Snervely sits on a pile of feces on your brain floor. It is many times his body size and comically so, if your sense of humor goes that way. .

"Oh, Snervely, you're really going to need to clean that up."

"Fnnerrr!" says Snervely. He opens a zipper in his abdomen and pulls out a broom. But the broom is as filth splattered as the floor.

"You know what, never mind," says Badbones. "We'll just leave a little present for the night custodian. They can clean up this space, right? And speaking of space, our next story takes us into outer space!"

Snervely opens another zipper sewn into his leg and pulls out a tiny, bloody envelope. He hands it to Professor Badbones.

"What have we here! Some fan mail?" Badbones waves the letter, showing off its pages. "Thick! Perhaps there is a photo or two! Some fan art!"

His eyes scan down. "Hmm. It's from the esteemed publisher of this fine volume, Snervely. Interesting they would have you give it to me rather than just deliver it themselves." Badbones puts on his bifocals and scans the first couple of pages. "It appears they have some "notes" about our segments. So we'll take a look, dear reader! While you all read the next gripping tale, about spaceships, I will wade through some twenty odd pages of printed e-mail corporate-ese. I'm not sure which of us will be less entertained! Hee hee hee!"

Badbones waves you to turn the page.

THAT TERRIFYING SWEETNESS

As the spaceship *Baltimore* settled into orbit around the pink planet, Captain Plank, myself, and the officers discussed our dwindling options. Low on fuel, resources, far from any more of our kind, we could either orbit this planet until the oxygen recyclers ran out of power, and become a floating museum of hubris, or take the *Baltimore*, never designed for planetary landing, into a controlled crash on the strange planet, chosen as the most likely to be habitable of the planets we could reach. We already knew it was swarming with life, but of what kind we knew not, intelligent or not, and we'd already lost all our sub ships to the infestation.

The officers were becoming lax in their professionalism, morose, cynical, morbid in their humor. There was talk of fermenting the dead into alcohol and having one last blow out party before we opened up the airlocks to suffocate ourselves. The doctor joked of letting us all succumb to the infestation, thus improving our odds of survival, albeit not in our current form.

In the far corner of the table, partially in shadow, sat Science Officer Loggenheim, batshit crazy/brilliant/weird/socially retarded old Loggenheim, once found masturbating in the space suit closet even though he was one of the few crewmembers with a private cabin. Loggenheim sat in the dark end of the table, silent, save for the cracks of pistachio shells being pried apart, taking it all in. We'd just tightened our food rations a third time but somehow he still always had his little bowl of pistachios. His room must have had crates of them. Loggenheim took it all in and waited for the frustrated lull in the conversation, the impotent, exhausted petering out of ideas, to make his move.

"It seems to me," he said, *crack*, pausing to lightly toss the green meat into his mouth, "we are forgetting a key third option. An option so obvious it is hiding in plain sight."

Everyone turned. Even the back room mutterers and mumblers were silent.

"The option of course being that we are all delusional. And what we perceive as reality is not our true reality."

I suddenly felt nauseous. Perhaps it was the anticipation. Perhaps it was all the stress we'd been under these months. I grabbed the napkin beneath my coffee mug and began to cough into it.

I felt like all eyes were on me then. Terrible timing. I tried to do a polite cough, but it just moved whatever was lodged in my lung to a still less comfortable place, so I coughed louder, involuntarily, working the thing out. I stood up and tried to get out the words to excuse myself but I simply coughed more. The thing was working its way out. The thing felt hard. Like a bone.

My mouth felt full of bone and I didn't know how I'd get it out. A bit of panic. It almost seemed like a, like a skull in there, it felt like my tongue was flitting over teeth, jaws, eye sockets.

I put my fingers in my mouth to try to crack it, break it apart and pull out the pieces, when it erupted and broke me apart. The skull was huge and had a—was it?—yes it was, a beret, and then I was dead.

Professor Badbones brushes the bits of meat from his jacket rather unsuccessfully. Then he pulls out his letter. brandishing it.

"A fucking letter! From the publisher!" he yells to the officers around the table, who are now standing and backing away, pistols drawn. "They don't even have the balls to call me. They give Snervely an e-mail printout to give to me."

Captain Plank's beam rips a hole through Badbones' jacket. Badbones looks up, not with pain, but with hurt feelings, as if they were at a party and Plank had walked off when Badbones was in mid-sentence to fix another Mojito. Badbones swats him, causing his torso to become a red smear against the wall of windows, making the stars outside turn pink.

The high-pitched scream, a woman's scream, pierces the silence. The scream comes not from Weapons Officer Sarah Teasley but from Loggenheim, his face contorted in existential fear. He's even dropped his pistachios.

"You think you've got problems?" Badbones asks. He flips through the well-worn pages. Portions are highlighted.

"They're not happy with the hosting bits. They're worried it's just filler. Why didn't they decide that shit before they hired me?"

"They say the jokes are tired. They don't like me popping out of the page. They told me to do that shit, to do the puns and now they're throwing me under the bus for it. I wanted to humorously dissect the themes of each story, but they said "No, too boring! Just do puns! Keep it quick!" and now they're saying the hosting bits aren't satisfying enough. No shit! They hate their own stupid previous notes and so that's my fault. Those cowardly fuckers.

"They said they didn't like that I kept appearing in the reader's brain, instead of different locations. They said no to other locations! They said no! Fine, they want me in a new location, here I am. In the short story. Let's see how they like that."

"And get this, Snervely, you're out. Nice way to tell you that, huh, buddy?" says Badbones to Snervely, who is trying to pry open a pistachio.

"They're swapping you out for a sexy cohost. They have one picked out, with big tits and a little black bats on her nipples or whatever and all that shit. Up the sex appeal for young men which they see as the audience. I thought they were worried about upping the page count and now they're telling me to add shit. They don't know what they fucking want, I tell you. Can prose even compete with visuals in the sex realm anyway? I don't care how well the author describes this chick—*Stiffany Corpse*—he can describe her ass and compare it to a bouncing peach every five lines but it ain't gonna compete with video. There's no scarcity of attractive women to look at. Have these dicks heard of the Internet?"

Badbones grabs the front of Sarah Teasley's uniform and tears it off. She covers her nakedness in fear. "Here's your sex appeal! Really adds to the story, huh?

"Jesus. I mean, give me a chance to get a rhythm going, to figure out what I do. Give me a chance! If it sucks, it sucks. Fine. It's a first draft. Fuck. Let's get some clear direction and do a second draft. Improve it. But no. You know these idiots are going to push me out and put this zombietits in my place. And probably some young hipster host that doesn't know a short story from his anus. Fuck. I passed up other offers for this shit. You know? I gotta think."

Professor Badbones walks to the outer wall and kicks a hole in it. With a whoosh, the air and all the people, the pistachios, Snervely, chairs, lamps are sucked out into the silence of space. Somewhere in the belly of the ship an alarm goes off. A hallway hisses as it seals automatically. Badbones does a running flip through the hole and follows the detritus.

Floating in space, falling to the pink planet, entering the atmosphere, Badbones' jacket, his khakis catch fire.

"Next up is a love story about midgets."

SNEEZY

The pale softness of your chin as it curves inward and then blossoms out into the red fullness of your lower lip: it is the most precious thing I have ever seen.

You have come into our lives with the fullness of womanhood; you have given us shiny woodtop tables, hot buttery cornbread, fresh clean ears. How we love you. Work in the mines seems less like drudgery, knowing you wait for us. We sing heigh-ho, heigh-ho with power and hope. Even Grumpy has been less irritable lately. We bring you diamonds. You bring us life.

Oh, how I love you. You have awakened me to life. We scrub the walkway together, scrubbing dirt, coal, and diamond dust from the cobblestones. Bluebirds fly around us singing. We kneel, facing each other, holding our scrub brushes. Circular motions. "This is how we did it at the castle," you say; your voice catching with a certain sadness. Your lowering eyelashes.

I ask you what it was like there. You shake your head softly. "I like it here much better, Sneezy," you say. I see your cleavage of breasts as they glow in the blouse. They are magic. They sway like apples—no, softer. They sway like boughs of leaves against your strong arms, as your hands work with the brush. I see your fingernails, happy teeth on your fingers. Magic.

I sneeze in excitement and the brush escapes my grip. You laugh a peal of silver bells. You put your hands over mine, show me how to hold the brush. For the briefest moment your grip tightens. Doc walks up suddenly. "Snow White, would you like to go picking berries with us?" I grit my teeth.

You remove your hands softly, wipe the soap from them in the fat folds of your skirt. "That sounds like a wonderful idea," you say, your eyes on me. Your eyes are beautiful blue moons on white skies. "Do you want to come, Sneezy?"

You are afraid to show preference, at least so soon. But something special is implicit in your gaze. I feel it. We pick blackberries with my six brothers, but I put the most in your basket. The smell from the juice makes me sneeze. I try to hold it. I must be more cautious around you.

That night, I lay in the rocking chair. My brothers are asleep and snoring, sleeping in pots, pans, stairwells, rugs, and benches. You lay in the room above us, our beds have been slid together to fit the largeness of your body. Seven beds on which you lie. I look up at the wood rafters in the ceiling and wonder which part of your body is lying on my bed. Each possibility makes me fuzzy, from the nighttime black feathery softness of your hair to your toes: trembling pink and separate on your feet.

The room is alive with sound … crickets, snores, and wolves howling in the forest. My own heartbeat. Still, through these noises, I hear your breath on the pillow, tucked away and secret. It's a secret we share and keep from my brothers.

To simply hold your hand would be the grandest thing. To brush your hair behind your ears and kiss your temples. To hold the back of your neck in my hand and feel it in my palm and fingers.

Your breathing is faster now, higher. The sound of wet eyelids opening and closing. You are crying! I want to walk up the stairs and console you, but I am afraid. The loud snores of my brothers surround me, threateningly competitive or disapproving.

But the rare chance to be alone with you has opened up for me. It is our chance to get closer. I dream of evenings when the seven of us march down the hill, Doc, Grumpy, Happy, Sleepy,

Me, Bashful, and Dopey; whistling our song, and you will pause in your dishwashing and gaze out the kitchen window. Your ears will find my part in the harmony. Your eyes will look down the row of matching hats and pick me out special.

I slide quietly off the chair and hold it still so it doesn't rock. I tiptoe through the living room past Bashful and Dopey and up the stairs. Stepping over Happy on the third stair, my nose gets warm and tickly. Darn! I clasp my hands tight over my nose, my hands are barely big enough to hold it. It is big like a loaf of bread. I squeeze it tight, but the tickling feeling won't stop. If I sneeze, someone may wake up. I will lose my chance to be alone with you and soothe your crying, for surely anyone waking up will want to wake the others and join me.

I sneeze, but I hold it tight, so only a fragile "ksssh" escapes. Most of the force goes inward, giving me a headache. The sneeze is quiet but Happy stirs.

"Sneezy," he whispers, eyes fluttering awake. "What are you doing?"

"I ... left something upstairs, Happy. I'm sorry I woke you," I reply.

"Can I help you find it?" he asks, giving me a sleepy smile.

"No, no. Go back to sleep. I know where it is, thank you."

"Goodnight." Happy turns over and begins snoring again. If only I was like Happy, content with anything, perky and joyful as a flower or bluebird. But no, I need you so much it makes me itch. You stand before me in your blue dress, you are in my mouth and on the inside of my eyelids. You are all I think about.

I am right outside your door now. I place my ear against it. Your crying is still soft, yet faster. I hesitate, my heart sounds like it is firing gunshots, Kapow, clic, Kapow, clic, Kapow. It is roaring in my ears. How dare I knock? You simply want to be left alone. How dare I be so bold?

I am compelled. The ambiguous possibility that you may truly love me as I love you, it is overwhelming. I cannot fritter away my time in fear of error. The tiny tactical miscalculations to capture your heart are risks, but I must act.

The knock sounds huge in my ears, it echoes like a boulder falling in the diamond mine. KNOCK, Knock, knock, nok. I turn my head back wildly, but Happy is still snoring.

Your crying has paused, however. I press my ear against the door again. I hear the soft wet separation of lips, but no words. I stand in darkness, waiting.

My hand is raised to knock again when you speak. "Yes?" The syllable tastes like fresh milk to my ears.

"Dopey?" you ask. My heart sinks. Dopey! My mind crashes. Have I been a fool? Has Dopey truly been the object of your affections? His clumsy antics must have tripped your heart strings, while I was unawares. I have been an egotistical fool.

Wait. I have been silent. Naturally you would assume I am Dopey the mute, since I have been standing here dumb. I'm a paranoid fool. I sneeze in nervous relief.

"Sneezy?" you ask. My heart soars. Miracle of miracles. Magics of magic. Your lungs have contracted, sliding breath over the curve of your tongue, through lips that you have formed to sound my name.

I take a deep breath. "It is me."

"Come in," you say. I push the wide wooden door open. The walls are fresh white. At your feet, your blue dress hangs neatly on the headboard of Doc's bed, bisected in moonlight from the sole window.

You sit up from lying on your back, holding our sewn together sheets to your chest with naked arms. "Hi," you say, and wipe a tear from your eye with a delicate finger. You smile.

"I heard you crying," I say. I walk past the rows of beds to your face, looking to see where my bed is. It holds your calves. "What's wrong?"

"Nothing," you say. You lower your eyes.

"Snow White, please tell me. It will make you feel better," I say, impressed at my own boldness.

You inhale and the sheets rise. "Oh Sneezy, what will I

do?" You look into me.

"What do you mean?" I ask. I sit down on the mattress beside you.

"I can't live here forever. I can't hide. The queen wants to kill me," you say, closing your eyes.

"We will protect you," I say. "I will protect you."

This moves you; you place your hand on my head. "Thank you. I don't know where I'd be without you all," you say. "Dead in the forest, I guess." You nestle the sheet in your crossed arms. I can see your naked back, the pale smoothness as it curves inward and begins to divide into halved roundness.

"Oh Sneezy," you say. Your hand moves to wipe your eye, I see your shoulder blade move. "What can I do? I had dreams of living in a castle. Of love." You hug your knees, shoulders shaking with sobs. I put my hand on your fragile back.

I put my arms around you. I lay my head softly on the back of your neck so I can hear your skin. "I have those dreams," I say. Frightened with my forwardness, I add, "We all do."

You pause. Your curved back is like water. You touch my sleeve, then speak. "I saw a man on a horse, the week before I left the castle. A handsome man. Strong. He made me realize how lonely I was."

"Probably a pig trader," I say, strengthening my grip around you. "It's funny how things like that will wake you up."

"You should have seen him," you say. "He looked like a prince. I was so shy." You giggle. "I bet you've never been in such a situation."

"I have." I begin rubbing your back. Like you taught me. Circular motions.

"Mmmm," you say. Your head tilts back. "Sneezy, I should just run away. We should both run away. Somewhere far."

I have died. "Where would you like to go?" I ask, my hands move down your back.

"How about the sea?" you say. "I declare, Sneezy, you give the best massage. Must be those tiny hands of yours ..."

I sneeze quickly on your back, I didn't even know it was coming. You giggle. "You're so cute, Sneezy," you say, twisting your body around. "Let me wipe your nose with this sheet."

You hold my nose in sheet fingers. I feel through my head for things to say. You called me cute. Cute is good. Cute means attractive, handsome. "I hate sneezing so much," I say.

"Oh, I think it's cute," you say, slight upward curve of your lips. Your neck straightens to glide smoothly down the plane of your skin to the sheet at your chest. Your arms tilt back to prop you up.

I want to lie back in the mattress and melt. I want to jump on you. I want to talk until morning. I want—

"What do you want for breakfast tomorrow, Sneezy?" you ask.

"It doesn't matter," I reply. "Everything you cook is so delicious. But I want to talk about the Evil Queen. Are you still upset?"

"Oh, please." You smile. "I'm not that great of a cook. But I'm learning." You tighten the sheets around you and walk to the window; it bathes you in soft light. "What would you think of me being a ship's cook?" You look out the window as if it looks over the sea. "Oh, but women curse a ship ..."

"I would have you on my ship," I say, trying to sound casual. "I could be the captain of the ship." I jump off the bed and walk to your side by the window. Standing by you I am rather aware that my eyes are even with the beautiful roundness of your hips and bottom.

"I love the sea," you say. "But I only went there once when I was young." I see the underside of your chin framed between your breasts. I miss your shoulders.

There is a pause filled with awkward breathings. Your eyes look at me as if they want something. I want to put my hand on the small of your back.

You shiver from a cold draft. "It's getting late," you say. "Or should I say early?" Your toes curl against the wood floor. Pause.

You walk back to bed. I follow. I follow.

You sit on the mattress. "Are you feeling better?" I ask.

"Much better," you say. "Thank you for coming up here. I really appreciate it." You kiss me on the forehead. It feels warm and a little wet. "You helped me a lot." You move your legs softly back into the bed, under the sheets. Your toes graze my penis. You lay back. "Good night, Sneezy. Thanks again."

Your body lies flat on the mattress. I can hear your heartbeat. You lay your head back. I pat your foot. Warm. "Good night," I say. "Don't let everything worry you too much." I walk slowly away.

When I reach the door I hear you say, "We should do this again, Sneezy. Just us two."

"Yes, I would like that." I am swimming.

Just us two! I am swimming in warm water I cannot drown in. Your words are gold in the air. I repeat it with every step I take. Do it again. Just us two. Do it again. Just us two. We were talking, flirting, communication, bonding. Hooray! I step over Happy. I am Happy now, no, I am happier. I'm ecstatic. Ecstatic the dwarf.

In my chair, I pause to listen. I hear the steady breaths of your happy sleep. I have dried your tears. Do you dream of me?

I dream of you, though I stay awake. I sit in the rocking chair, shaking with energy. You and me. When the time is right, I will tell Doc I want my share of the diamonds. I will buy a ship.

Morning comes, but I am still not tired. My brothers and I ready for work, cheerfully. You descend the stairs like a queen. You cook us pancakes, my favorite. As we depart, you give me a wink.

A wink! Outside, the air is cool. We sing.

The mine is cool, too, but you keep me warm. We work. At lunch, we eat sandwiches unwrapped from cloth napkins.

"Things sure are better with Snow White around," Doc says, cleaning his glasses. He sits neatly on a rock with half a sandwich on his lap.

"She's b-beautiful," says Bashful, turning red.

Dopey nods eagerly, crumbs on his face.

"She cleans the house nicely," Sleepy says, then dozes off.

"A fair cook," Grumpy says.

"An excellent cook!" retorts Doc. "And an excellent cleaner! And pretty!"

This makes me angry. "She's not our maid," I say. "She's not our plaything. What about her life?"

"Who put the bee in your trousers?" Doc asks.

"I don't know," I say. "It's just that you all keep acting like she's our nanny or something."

"Now hold on here," says Doc. "We all think very highly of Snow White. We love her. What's gotten into you?"

"I don't know." I'm trembling. "This is crazy. What the hell are we doing? Why do we mine diamonds? What the hell do we use them for?"

A hush falls over them. Sleepy wakes up. Doc says, "Swearing is a—"

"Hell!" I scream. "Why are we wasting our lives in this damn forest? I can't believe this. I want to travel. I want to have sex!"

Their faces turn red. Doc is shaking in spasms. "Stop! Stop!"

"Does this have something to do with seeing Snow White last night?" Happy asks.

"What?" asks Doc.

Dopey shakes his fist.

"Y—you were with S—Snow White last night?" asks Bashful, dropping his sandwich.

"What happened?" Doc asks.

"Come on! Nothing happened," Grumpy yells. "She's a human, we're dwarves!"

"What happened?!!" Doc asks.

"We're going away," I say. I imagine you nodding your head as I say this, your teeth nibbling my ears. "I was meaning to wait

46

a few weeks, but what the hell. I want my share of the diamonds, Doc. Snow White and I are leaving." Everyone gasps in unison.

"You can't split up the group!" cries Doc.

"You fool!" Grumpy screams. "Snow White won't run away with you!"

"No, you're the fools!" I yell. Everyone is surrounding me, but I feel your hands on my shoulders.

Suddenly birds are flying around us, squirrels and rabbits are at our feet.

"What is it?" asks Doc. Birds are pulling at his collar.

"Something must be wrong!" I yell.

"Snow White!" cries Sleepy.

"Another crisis, great," mutters Grumpy.

We jump on deer and hurry to our cottage. My blood is boiling. Outside I see you with an ugly hag. You bring an apple to your lips, then faint.

Grumpy, Dopey, and I chase after the hag, pelting her with rocks and diamonds. We scatter through the forest after her. I see her behind a tree.

"Too late, too late," she cackles. "Your precious Snow White is dead, and only a kiss from her true love can save her!"

"Hag!" I scream, throwing two stones. They pass through her as she fades away. I run back to you. You lie on the stones we once scrubbed.

"She's dead," says Doc. He's crying.

We take your body out to the forest. We put you in a glass coffin because we can't bear the thought of burying you. Everyone is crying. Dopey sprinkles daisy petals around the coffin.

We sit in the kitchen, mourning. We eat supper, the last one you had prepared for us. I think of you lying in the flat coffin. I can't hear you breathing. Do you dream of me?

Doc takes me aside. "Let's just forget about the little incident in the mine today. Is that fine with you?"

"Yes."

But they all succumb to sleep. That night, I take a modest bag of diamonds, a candle, and some food and clothes and hurry into the forest.

Your dreams are in my dreams. The night is alive with it. The air woos in it. I come into the clearing where you lie under glass. I see the reflection of myself and the candle next to you. You look preserved, like cake. I don't like it. I am anxious to revive you. I miss your eyes.

With great effort, I push the coffin open. Your hair moves with quick breezes. I can see the salt air blowing through your hair. Your face on a backdrop of blue waves. The sun will tan your skin.

Your skin is still soft. You are beautiful and fragile. Like the glass coffin.

"I am here," I say.

The pale softness of your chin as it curves inward and then blossoms out into the red fullness of your lower lip: it is the most precious thing I have ever seen.

I kiss you. Your lips are cold, but I feel a glimmer of warmth.

I sit up and look at your eyelids, waiting for them to flutter open. The bag of diamonds sits in daisy petals. The boat will be big and brown, with sails as fair as your skin. I will wear a captain's hat.

I wait. I wait for you to breathe. To move a finger. I kiss you again. And again. I kiss your neck, your forehead, your cheek. I kiss your hands and your arms. I kiss your fingers.

Dawn comes, I hear the distant sound of horse's hooves churning fallen leaves. It is getting louder. A man yells "faster" to his steed.

My throat feels pulled. My tears wet your face. I kiss your elbows. I kiss your feet.

INTERMISSION

"That was a sweet little tale of unrequited desire, don't you think?" asks Professor Badbones.

He is in a forest clearing, sitting on a log around a little fire, eating roast deer leg. Beside him, tied up, is the rest of the deer, unroasted, pleading. Littered around are elephant bones, a mermaid's tail, and a set of large, half-eaten mouse ears.

"Please, please, sir—" says the deer.

"Quiet please," says the host. "Unless you want to end up like your rabbit friend. By the way, how do you like my bunnyskin cap? Better than the beret? Hee hee hee!" He then pauses a moment, self consciously, and quickly adds, in a rushed mumble, "This is a reference to Thumper, from the animated film Bambi. These references may be lost on younger readers since that movie has somewhat fallen from the limelight."

"If you ask me, Snow White shoulda banged all the dwarves. Simultaneously!" says a woman's voice, sexy and husky. The fire flickers. "Princes are soooo boring!"

She erupts up from the fire hugging her black motorcycle. The cycle lands on a tree, toppling it, and disappears in the woods, engine revving, until it returns doing a quick circle around the campfire and ending with a sliding stop that deposits a wavelet of dirt on Badbones' loafers.

Her long corpse-white legs peel off the bike and she removes her blood red helmet. Black hair spills out and down like pretty girls' hair spills out of helmets in countless movies and TV shows. She wears blood red shorts with rips and holes likes she's fought off a fellow zombie or two. Wide hips leading up to a belly button on her narrow waist. A red leather jacket, open, reveals black suspenders leading up and strategically covering the nipples of her bare breasts. Black eyes and bruise colored lips.

"I'm Stiffany Corpse. And this is my cohost, Professor Badbones."

"I am not your cohost." snipes Badbones. "I am the host and you are *my* cohost. And I know how to introduce myself. I don't need to be introduced. Have you even been reading this book?"

"You can't have one cohost. Cohost implies two hosts on equal footing," she says. If Badbones had cheeks they would flush red, because he knows she is correct. The focus of this paragraph moves to Stiffany's body as she brushes dirt off her moon-white thighs, her stomach, and her breasts, restlessly bobbling, springing, like they have ADHD and they can't decide where to settle, suspenders sliding like the whole confabulation is going to fall apart, but it doesn't.

"Our next story is called Frequently Asked Questions," Stiffany say. "My only question is if this short story collection is going to get any better!" She gives you a wink.

"I thought they said no puns!" protests Badbones.

Stiffany laughs. "Rules are made to be broken!" she says, and guns the engine causing another stream of dirt and stones to fly across Badbones' shins.

Stiffany's chalk white midriff ripples some more and then bulges. Stiffany pauses in pain just as Badbones rips out of her stomach. "This short story shows guts!" Badbones says with a leer, as he drops to the ground. He's holding her intestines in his hands. A kidney, or maybe a liver (I'm not a medical doctor) drops onto the grass. "Anyone for jump rope? Or should I say, jump intestines heee hee hee ooo …" Badbones doubles over in pain.

"This short story has balls!" Stiffany says, as she rips out the crotch of Badbones' corduroys. Something about the cracking of bones reminds you of the time you cracked a Sand dollar as a child. You don't hear much about Sand dollars anymore. You wonder if they are extinct, or at least endangered.

Badbones erupts from a tree. "The author is going out on a limb! We can do this all day. It's getting tired."

"I agree. It's totally tired. You should stop doing it."

"I will. I'll invent a new type of entrance, so you'll have a new thing you can steal from me."

The deer takes the opportunity the distraction affords to chew on the rope tethering his neck to the tree. He is agile, and can steal away quietly, even just on his three legs. He chews quickly and quietly.

FREQUENTLY ASKED QUESTIONS

Who are you?

We are NeighborBanke™, a new kind of financial services provider providing financial services and solutions where you live and work. We are more than just a bank. We are NeighborBanke™.

Why are you chasing me with an ax?

Whether it's through our best-in-class "Fee? What's a Fee?" checking™ or iHaveADream Savings™, we are committed to serving you, the customer. Perhaps we are not chasing you with an ax, but running to fight off an attacker on the other side of you. Or perhaps we are about to slaughter a chicken that we will cook for you at a friendly backyard barbecue. Now, would your old bank do that? We are more than just a bank. We are NeighborBanke™. Was this answer helpful? Please rate it from 1-5 stars.

You broke into my bedroom and attacked me. There is no attacker in this room. Just my wife. There is no chicken. I've never even heard of NeighborBanke™. Please stop attacking me!

Your privacy is important to us. You may have been selected for one of our promotions due to your interest in similar products and services. At NeighborBanke™, help is never more than a click away! If you wish to opt out, simply log on to NeighborBanke™ with your log in and password and select the tab SERVICE, select the choice PROMOTIONS, and select OPT IN and then CANCEL and then CONFIRM. If you don't have a login and password, simply click on CREATE ACCOUNT.

How am I supposed to get to my computer when I am fending you off with this nightstand?

At NeighborBanke™ you can always talk to a real live Service Advocate via e-mail, instant messaging, or phone, 24 hours a day, 7 days a week. No Internet or phone? Simply put down the nightstand and say "NEED HELP."

Need he—owww! Oh you fucker! You chopped my arm! You lied to me! You tricked me, you fucker!

We at NeighborBanke™ strive to exceed your expectations. Whether you're at work, in your bedroom, or running down the hall attempting to lock yourself in your child's room. We are everywhere you want to be. We are more than just a bank. We are NeighborBanke™.

Don't come in here! Don't come in here, or I swear I'll use this baseball bat on you!

Our mobile ATMs are tamper proof, water proof, shock proof, and bomb proof up to three hundred tons of explosive pressure. Your money is safe, although you may not be! Have you seen our viral marketing videos? "You do the grilling while we help you make a killing™." Send us your favorite grilling recipes and you may win exclusive discounts on popular products and services!

You are malfunctioning. How do I shut you off?

In the unlikely event you need to report a broken mobile ATM, please contact our service advocate at the number given.

What is the number for the service advocate?

Please refer to previous question where it was given. We are a different kind of bank. We are NeighborBanke™.

You never gave us the number of a service advocate. You are wrong.
We are sorry we were unable to help you further with this problem. Would you like us to put you in contact with a service advocate directly through our mobile ATM?

Yes!
So that we can put you in touch with the right service advocate, please state your problem.

"Mobile ATM is trying to kill us."
I heard, "Question about our CD rates." Was that correct?

No! "Mobile ATM attacking us with ax!"
Our service advocates are currently vigorously advocating for other service members. In the meantime, our mobile ATMs can help you with general questions from interest checking to a full suite of retirement services. Please move your bed away from the door and let us do the rest!

I am a service advocate! I order you to shut yourself off.
You are not wearing the requisite NeighborBanke™ badge. Nor the leaf green service shirt. You are lying. You are making me angry.

-Honey, you're making it angry.
-No shit! What do you think I should—
-Let me—Let me—in its own language—
-Fine honey. If you think—be my guest—
-We love NeighborBanke™. Is there any account we can sign up for where you will stop providing your ax swinging service? It does not serve our needs at this time.

Certainly! We are proud to offer three tiers of service to service three levels of need. They are good neighbor, close neighbor, and close neighbor-elite.

Which tier of service will you stop coming after us with an ax?
We're glad you "axed!" First, for your security: what is your favorite movie? What is your childhood best friend? What is your mother's maiden name?

What? What about my mother's maiden name? It's Brownlee.
Accessing. Margaret Brownlee Weiss. 327 Lindon Road. Thank you for the referral. You are eligible to win a book of NeighborBanke™ Grilling Recipes, sent in by customers just like you! You do the grilling while we help you make a killing. NeighborBanke™. We're almost ready to bust the door down to provide you with savings!

-It's going to attack my mom!
-Help! Help!
-Don't yell out the window, honey. There's more of them in the yard.
-God. And in the DeFalque's yard.
-As long as—stay quiet honey. Keep Cody quiet. It is having trouble with the door. As long as—Wait, I think it's leaving.
NeighborBanke™ is with you 24/7 and everywhere you want to be. We strive to provide a full range of services to serve the whole family, from providing Mom a low interest loan for a kitchen renovation to our Kid's Money Klub for your son. Speaking of which, we are expanding our services through the bathroom wall right now to make ourselves more accessible to your son who is hiding in the closet. Pardon our progress!

-Shit. Cody! Cody!!!
-There's a hole in the back of the closet. It must have grabbed him
—

–Cody!!

We apologize for any inconvenience. Please understand it is always our policy to follow all rules and regulations. You were the one who wants us to make a killing while you do the grilling. Killing is murder. We are duty bound to stop you and your money from making a killing. It is what a good neighbor must do. We are NeighborBanke™. We are a different kind of bank. Heroic, even.

–"Make a killing" is a figure of speech you worthless piece of shit. I will ass rape you and the worthless overpaid marketing shits that wrote your piece of shit brain you fucking fuck and the CEO's that approved you.

If what you say is true, why did you try to turn me off and therefore, kill me? Just as we provide overdraft protection for a nominal fee, we also must protect you and your savings, from your killing. Not even the baseball bat you are hitting the door with can stop us from providing our five-star service.

–Open this door! Can you give us Cody? Cody, can you hear me? Aaaaiiiggghhhh!!!!

We admit it. Our dedication to service sometimes makes our customers a little crazy. Send in a funny viral video about your banking relationship with NeighborBanke™ and you may win a—

We have a video. We have a viral video for you. Come out into the hall so we can give you our viral video.

Would your old bank come into your hall to receive a viral video you have made about your banking relationship with us? We're more than just a bank. We're—

Now!!—aiiiggghhhh! Die die die!

I'm sorry, it appears you may have mistakenly jostled us with your baseball bat and we are partially wedged face down in the stairwell. Pardon the interruption in world class service while we right ourself.

-Cody! I'm here—Shit.
-What is it, honey? What's wrong?
-Cody! What did you do to him?

At NeighborBanke™, we believe "You're the Banker." You can now make deposits and withdrawals through customers just like you! Simply put your NeighborBanke™ ATM card in Cody's mouth-hole and type your personal identification number on the keypad in his abdominal cavity. Envelope-free deposits and withdrawals can be made through the anus. But caution! Withdrawals from our bio-ATMs may contain bio-fluids. This feature is still in beta and only available in select markets.

You're stuck, you stupid fuck. You can't get up. And I will demolish you. Wire by wire you piece of shit fuck.

In life you have to prepare for the ups, and the downs. With our market protection CD you can earn a safe return in any environment. Look inside your son's anus compartment for an exclusive color brochure with deals in your area!

I will keep beating you. I will keep beating you with everything in this house until you break. What do you think of that?

We regret that this mobile ATM is temporarily out of service. Please note that as part of our MyMoneyNow™ pledge we have dispatched three more mobile ATM's to your house. We are ringing your doorbell right now. We are at your backdoor. We are climbing on your deck. We are coming into your basement. We are everywhere you want to be. We are NeighborBanke™. You focus on the grilling, let us make a killing

killing killing killing killing killing killing killing killing killing
killing killing killing killing killing killing killing killing killing
killing killing killing killing killing killing killing killing killing
killing killing killing killing killing killing killing killing killing
killing killing killing killing killing killing killing killing killing
killing killing killing killing killing killing killing killing killing
killing killing killing killing killing killing killing killing killing
killing killing killing killing killing killing killing killing killing
killing killing killing killing killing killing killing killing killing
killing killing killing killing killing killing killing killing killing
killing killing killing killing killing killing killing killing killing
killing killing killing killing killing killing killing killing killing
killing killing killing killing killing killing killing killing killing
killing killing killing killing killing killing killing killing killing
killing killing killing killing killing killing killing killing killing
killing killing killing killing killing killing killing killing killing
killing killing killing killing killing killing killing killing killing
killing killing killing killing killing killing killing killing killing
killing killing killing killing killing killing killing killing killing
killing killing killing killing killing killing killing killing killing
killing killing killing killing killing killing killing killing killing
killing killing killing killing killing killing killing killing killing
killing killing killing killing killing killing killing killing killing
killing killing killing killing killing killing killing killing killing
killing killing killing killing killing killing killing killing killing
killing killing killing killing killing killing killing killing killing
killing killing killing killing killing killing killing killing killing
killing killing killing killing killing killing killing killing killing
killing killing killing killing killing killing killing killing killing
killing killing killing killing killing killing killing killing killing
killing killing killing killing killing killing killing killing killing
killing killing killing killing killing killing killing killing killing
killing killing killing killing killing killing killing killing killing
killing killing killing killing killing killing killing killing killing
killing killing killing killing killing killing killing killing killing

killing killing killing killing killing killing killing killing killing
killing killing killing killing killing killing killing killing killing
killing killing killing killing killing killing killing killing killing
killing killing killing killing killing killing killing killing killing
killing killing killing killing killing killing killing killing killing
killing killing killing killing killing killing killing killing killing
killing killing killing killing killing killing killing killing killing
killing killing killing killing killing killing killing killing killing
killing killing killing killing killing killing killing killing killing
killing killing killing killing killing killing killing killing killing
killing killing killing killing killing killing killing killing killing
killing killing killing killing killing killing killing killing killing
killing killing killing killing killing killing killing killing killing
killing killing killing killing killing killing killing killing killing
killing killing killing killing killing killing killing killing killing
killing killing killing killing killing killing killing killing killing
killing killing killing killing killing killing killing killing killing
killing killing killing killing killing killing killing killing killing
killing killing killing killing killing killing killing killing killing
killing killing killing killing killing killing killing killing killing
killing killing killing killing killing killing killing killing killing
killing killing killing killing killing killing killing killing killing
killing killing killing killing killing killing killing killing killing
killing killing killing killing killing killing killing killing killing
killing killing killing killing killing killing killing killing killing
killing killing killing killing killing killing killing killing killing
killing killing killing killing killing killing killing killing killing
killing killing killing killing killing killing killing killing killing
killing killing killing killing killing killing killing killing killing
killing killing killing killing killing killing killing killing killing
killing killing killing killing killing killing killing killing killing
killing killing killing killing killing killing killing killing killing
killing killing killing killing killing killing killing killing killing
killing killing killing killing killing killing killing killing killing
killing killing killing killing killing killing killing killing killing
killing killing killing killing killing killing killing killing killing

killing Thank you for your patience.

INTERMISSION

The downstairs guest bath is clean and bland like the bathrooms in many American suburban homes. Off-white porcelain and light woods. The sink is designed to evoke a peasant well, complete with faux country pump handle. Beside that are toothbrushes, a rolled tube of toothpaste for guests (Colgate Cinnamon), a chrome bar affixed to the wall which holds a forest green towel and a matching washcloth, which is folded and placed diagonally over the towel.

The only thing unusual is the large skeleton soaking in the bathtub. Professor Badbones lays there, no fleshy finger tips to get pruny, eyes fixed on his phone. He is playing a game. Then he pauses his game and checks his e-mail. Then he returns to the game. He gets fed up with the game and then checks a blog he likes to see if it is updated. It isn't. Of course, he would have gotten an e-mail if it had updated, anyway, but sometimes there's a delay to the e-updates he has registered for so he checks the blog as well.

Badbones looks up and sees you there.

"What the fuck are you doing here?"

He waits for your reply but there is none forthcoming.

"Get the fuck out! This is not a funny hosting bit. This is me taking a bath. This is a private moment! Go! Go!"

He picks up the washcloth and throws it at you.

"Who even sent you here? The editors?"

"I was fired. Fired! I'm not the host anymore, okay? Go

listen to Stiffany. Did she send you here?"

You look at Badbones naked in the tub. Without his clothes he is just a skeleton.

"Don't look at that. Why are you looking at that? Go ahead, get an eyeful. What is your deal? Go. You shouldn't even be here. This isn't a joke. Seriously. Just go."

"No I'm not going to introduce the next story. I don't know and I don't care. I'm trying to figure out what to do with the rest of my life. I was never even in to horror hosting. I don't give a shit about that stuff. I just kept getting pushed into it, pushed into it. Because everyone sees me as a disgusting skeleton, I guess."

He gets out of the tub and dries himself. It feels weirdly intimate being in there with him.

In the eat-in kitchen there is a laptop and a cup of coffee. The laptop shows a job hunting site.

"You just send these résumés into a black hole. Especially in this economy. I don't know if anyone reads them. If I could just get an interview, if they could just meet me!"

Badbones takes a sip of the coffee. It spills through his ribs and onto the crotch of his pants.

"Great! Just great!"

The phone rings. It is Badbones' brother, Owen. Owen works in medical supplies and Badbones is considering applying to this company. He gets the ins and outs of what it is like to work there, and if they are hiring, and what they are looking for.

While they talk, Badbones takes out a cigarette. The smoke seeps out through his eyes, his ear holes, his ribs.

His call waiting beeps. It is his wife, Dana, calling him to say ballet class is over and she is swinging by a restaurant with the kids and does he want anything. She's thinking Mexican.

He looks up and notices you again. "You're still here? Does this excite you? Do you enjoy the schadenfreude of seeing a quote unquote entertainer in humiliating circumstances? I bet you just love that shit. Fine! Go masturbate to my misery for all I care. Let you forget about your own. I could kill you or maim you in some funny way, pop out of your skull or something but I seriously can't be bothered. Just go.

"Go!"

LARGE BREASTED NINJAS
OF ALTAIR SEVEN
❧

OLD FARTS OF 2138

I only virt two hours a day, three on weekends. It's not that I don't like it. It's that I like it too much. I'm retired. I live alone. There is nothing to stop me from virting until I'm hungry or fall asleep or die. You've seen this in the news. It takes discipline to not be an addict.

Other old farts like me—creaky, crackly, rheumy-eyed, half deaf, floppy skinned, no money for gene replenishment—often opt for the surgery, their brains removed and plopped in a little vat and wired to live in a virtual adventure for the rest of its life. Brainhousing. It has its advantages. It is exciting, and cheap. You don't have to pay to keep up your apartment, or stay fed, or get surgery for cataracts, cancer, kidney transplants, skin replacement, etc. You don't have to suffer the indignity of aging, or even of having a physical self at all. You can have a body like your twenty-four-year-old self. Or better. You can trade in your one room shitpartment for a castle on a cloud or a secret agent HQ in a volcano. You can be a superhero, detective, spy, magnate or rock star riding unicorns or young virgins or both at the same time, ejaculating rainbows. Pass on that money saved to your kids, the real ones, not the virt ones, if you had virt ones—if that was your thing, a virt family. Everybody wins.

Not me. A picture: me walking down the street carrying bags of groceries, the bag handles cutting into my fingers, especially the one with the milk. Me walking unsteadily but trying to keep those muscles moving, moving, getting looked at if at all by bewildered or pitying eyes. I work hard to enjoy real life, in all its hot, crowded misery. Real life is what you make it. I'd say I'm stubbornly old-fashioned but all my friends my age are brainhoused. I'm just stubbornly ... what?

Maybe it's that as good as virtualing is, it's just not quite the same. There's the subtle things of real life that the programmers miss. The feel of the stubble left after my shaky job shaving my saggy chin. A rip in the wallpaper above my bathtub that sort of looks like a cat. The variety of human faces on the street. The feel of my nose hairs when I'm breathing. The texture of pizza reheated in my toaster oven that is partially burnt and partially still cold. The way, as I'm sitting on the sofa, my great-great-grands balance themselves as they climb up my back before they get scolded by my great-grands. The mixture of love, pity, horror, irritation, condescension, and still more love in my oldest daughter Justine's voice towards me. Maybe it's that they don't put enough pain and disappointment in the virts, so the pleasure isn't as sweet, it's unearned.

But they absolutely nailed the smell of fresh mown grass, and sunsets. I'll give them that. And give them a few years and they'll probably nail everything else, even nose hairs. (Assuming you configure your avatar to have them. And why would you?)

BEDTIME RITUALS 2012

While my wife cleaned the kitchen, I would bathe Justine and Britney and get them in their jammies. I loved the smell of their just dried hair and the loudness of their excited voices. Even their whispers were loud.

Often the backs of their arms would be dry so I would put lotion on them. I would also lotion their feet in between the toes and that would make them giggle. Then they would want to lotion my arms, my toes, with their tiny clumsy hands. Then my wife or I would read picture books and tell them a made up story where they were the stars—where they save an injured elf, befriend a talking tiger, find a treasure or convince a mean witch to be kind.

The stories would get more convoluted as the girls got old enough to start inserting their own parts. Justine would frequently try to remove drama, while my youngest, Britney, would try to add to it. If I said "They walked into the deep dark cave," then Justine would add "and then they pulled the flashlight out of their pockets" or even "But then Justine and Britney decided not to go into the cave and just went home" and I would adjust the story so that when they got home there was an invitation to a birthday party at a princess's castle. And Justine would add that it was also her birthday party. And also that she was a princess too. But then once at the multiple-princess birthday party Britney would say "But then a monster came and ate Justine up and Britney super kicked it's booty and called the police and they put it in the jail." So I would have to get an a-story and b-story going to satisfy my divergent audience.

After the story, I would carry each child from my bed to theirs. Over the years, new ways were invented. The methods, roughly in order of invention, were: on the hip, on the shoulders, in the arms like a little baby, flying like Tinkerbell (where I would hold them up by their bellies sort of like a waiter with a beer tray but with various dramatic swoops and soars and dips added, and also singing songs from *Peter Pan*) (also in this position they would always enjoy pausing to slap the pull rope to the attic door), upside down, and lastly holding their arms and my wife holding their legs and swinging them along the way— the hammock.

Carrying them there's an awareness they are growing and one day they will be too big and one time will be the last time you carry them ever. And maybe you should get video of carrying them, but then you get sidetracked and suddenly you realize that last time was a year ago.

Also, collapsing into bed with my wife. The kids are finally asleep. A sweet sense of fatigue and accomplishment. We did it. We are good parents. We are productive members of society. We earned this. This time in bed, canoodling to bad TV in the luxury of 800 thread count sheets. A happy marriage is another thing that feels like it will last forever. Those stable middle years with their quiet joys that feels like it will never end. But it ends. My wife had the thoughtless temerity to pass before me. One of those antibiotic-proof superbugs of 2109.

TELL ME ABOUT ME

My virt service uploaded a new virtual for me that was strangely untitled. The info pane said the game creates itself around my wants and needs and then gives a title to itself. It is a new and radical insanely great technology, in a long line of new and radical insanely great technologies.

It accesses your ident, your neurological activity, your buying patterns, viewing habits, your dreams, your obsessive thoughts, your unconscious yearnings. It tracks what your eyes linger on. Then after a few days of that it creates a virt just for you. You're a 1940s detective. Or you're a vampire. Or you're a 1940s detective vampire who lives in your hometown the way you remember it when you were seven, mixed partially with a favorite sitcom.

The character of loved ones may appear, or not. Or amalgams, or those imaginary dream friends that have an intensity like maybe you knew them in a past life.

I was apprehensive but vanity got the best of me. What would this machine tell me about me? What world did I secretly crave?

A POIGNANT THOUGHT NO LONGER RELEVANT OR APPLICABLE

People would always videotape and photograph the big things. The birthdays, the weddings, the vacations to China. But it's really the small things you want to remember. Oh to have video of my grandfather's gentle rants from his recliner chair, or video of me telling my girls stories and their little additions, or what my old office looked like with all that old movie history, or of the morning conversations with my wife while she brushed her teeth and I was in the shower.

Of course, now they have cameras the size of pin pricks, people can record their whole lives, and do. But back then cameras were the size of your hand, and you couldn't get it all, and even if you could you'd never have time to watch it.

BRILL CREAM AND OCTOPUS ARMS

While the blank virt did its analyzing, I decided I'd venture outside into the fat thick of people and get a coffee. People on the street looked at me the way I used to look at the very old. "I am young. Being your age is so very far away, it will never get there." It does. "When I'm the old I'll be healthier, happier, more successful, more famous." I thought the exact thing at your age and I hope you have better luck with that. "How do you live like that, so old?" You'd be surprised what you adjust to. "Why don't you just brainhouse? Or better yet, die?" You'd be surprised what you adjust to.

I always swore I would stay young at heart. I would never be an old person who couldn't understand youth, or youth culture. I didn't want to be like my mom who never understood e-mail. I'd never want to be frozen in time, like my granddad, his hair brillcreamed into a pompadour, leather glasses protector in his shirt pocket, the waist of his pants almost up to his armpits. Ranting about what happened to music, that it's not music anymore, or the gays, or the blacks, or the kids with their pants so low. As a kid I thought, when I'm old I will know to wear my pants at the height that is currently in fashion. But now, here I am, and the kids didn't wear any pants at all. They wear those floating holograms that blur their nakedness, or some other damn thing.

I squeezed into the coffee shop and ordered a latte with anti-anxiety. The girl who served me, maybe twenty, had a genetically added penis hanging off the side of her forehead that she kept tucking behind her ear. She was cute, it was a cute gesture, but still, the penis, why? And the other things. The gills. A cat tail. Five eyes. Octopus arms. My great-great-grand had asked for night vision eyes and retracting claws. It was what all the kids asked for.

I moved to a table to sip my coffee. Young people looked at me almost afraid I would start talking to them. The truth is I did want to talk to them. I needed people. I needed to talk. But I just couldn't offer what they needed. I guess I spoke too slowly and softly. Maybe my tongue wasn't what it used to be and was too slurry. Maybe my presence reminded them of death. Maybe they thought I was selfish to still be here, taking up precious resources. "Nice day," I offered. There was no answer. Even when I flattered, when I asked them questions about themselves, everything I tried, their eyes were rolling, stealing knowing glances with their friends. I feared/suspected/knew my daughters and my grand-kids and great-grands and great-greats felt that way. I was a waste of space. At least until the anti-anxiety latte kicked in.

I needed people my own age. But they weren't to be seen out in the world much. Most of them were brainhoused. I wasn't ready yet.

ANOTHER POIGNANT THOUGHT NO LONGER RELEVANT OR APPLICABLE

I had always loved movies. Movies, movies. The old musty smell of the theaters. The popcorn, the giant soda cups, sticky floors. The parting of light in the darkness. It made me want to be a filmmaker, making the challenging art films I loved. Really boring down into the human condition. It didn't work out that way, but I did become a cinematographer specializing in food commercials. I could really capture the softness of partially melted ice cream, the golden bubbles in beer, the moistness in brownies.

Of course they don't have commercials anymore, not the kind you just watch, anyway, and food is animated in 3-D now, such an easy thing any four-year-old can do it. It looks better than my work. If I tried to show my work to somebody, the proudest moments of my career, it would be met with pity, confusion. My hard earned skill is not a skill anymore.

I kept a list of the top one hundred movies in my head. Constantly refined it. A pantheon. A permanent hall of the timeless classics. To my surprise, not only did my favorite movies not survive the test of time, neither did the artform itself. People today have never seen a movie. They live them, in virts. You tell them about movies, about the excitement of a scene, of Al Pacino in the Godfather, and they stare at you blankly. Movies are virts where you are not allowed to talk to anybody or touch anything. It's dead. It's as dead as vaudeville. It reminded me of reading how, before the advent of fast photography, there was a profession called sports illustrator—people who would illustrate key moments of a sports event for newspapers. (Ah, newspapers.)

And the sad thing was even I had changed. The other day I tried to watch *Casablanca*. And I was bored.

I wanted to kiss Ingrid Bergman myself. Or perhaps I wanted to be on the tarmac kissing my wife again. Or both, overlapping, simultaneously, like a double-exposed photograph,

73

back when they had film.

DING

I got an alert that my personal virt was now ready for me. I got home and got comfortable. Made sure I was hydrated and fed and set the timer for two hours. I turned on the monitors—the ones that checked my heart rate, blood flow—you'd be surprised at the deaths from deep vein thrombosis from virting. And still there'd be stories of people hacking their virtuals to never kick them out and eventually they'd die of thirst. They'd be discovered later, always, it seems, partially eaten by their cat.

I slid the jack into the port on my neck. YOUR GAME: the screen said. And then LARGE BREASTED NINJAS OF ALTAIR SEVEN.

Really? I thought. I was offended. I'm an educated person. I'm well read. I've read James Joyce. Ulysses. Kafka. Chekov. I adore Bergman films. Kubrick. Altman. Jacques Tati, Tarkovsky, Satyajit Ray, dammit. And you throw this shit at me? Large Breasted Ninjas of Altair Seven? Is this a joke? Do you just give this to every old man and assume it will push their buttons? If I was a woman, would it have been some Cinderella Vampire High School Romance Dance Contest Cooking Show? Why do they insult us? Fuck this.

WHITE BALANCE

Another memory: calling a girl you liked and then hanging up in mortal fear. This was before caller ID, e-mail, vid chat, psychic telesonar message. You would just do it to hear her hello, and hang up, and then you would fall into the sound of her voice for a while, and just that hello would be enough, enough running around room for your heart to play in for a while, with its hopes and anticipations.

Another memory. Being bored as a teenager. Lying on my

bed. Hungry for something but not knowing what. Being bored and trapped in the suburbs. Pre-Internet. We were still information poor. We would need to get a ride to the store to pick up a stinking magazine, if there was even a magazine you cared about. And when you finally did find something you liked —a song on a mixed tape given to you by a girlfriend, that song would grow to be your own world. You would cling to it, listen to it over and over, you would master it.

Now information is a constant waterfall. We are being waterboarded with information. And not that it's bad. Truth is, there are too many good things for me to read, watch, listen to. I miss the childhood of wanting more. You invented it on your own. My friends and I picked up a camera and made our own movie. Something silly about ninjas. Vampires. I would go on to make short films with my daughters, too. Fairies, pirates, treasure. Britney's favorite trick was shaking the camera to simulate an earthquake or a car crash.

HIT START

Ok, let's just give these large breasted ninjas a shot. Let's just do it. I mindslide the cursor over and hit START and:

A bunch of college students are looking at me. I'm in a classroom. I'm teaching the class. I'm teaching a class on film. By the attire it's somewhere late 1990s. One of the kids wears a shirt of my favorite band. The lecture I am giving is just spilling out of me, the virt is putting the words in my mouth, words I've thought but it's making them more elegant, organizing them better. But there's little holes where I can add my own bits, or gently steer the stream of words.

After the class students linger. They ask me questions. They have wide eyes. They are interested. Then I'm running off to an appointment. A racquetball game with my friend, a fellow professor, Todd. As I change into my gym clothes I admire my body. My muscular thighs. Washboard abs. Sturdy genitals. I take a glance at my face in the mirror. Nice muscular jaw that I never had in real life, but still, sensitive eyes. Black full hair without a touch of grey.

I never liked sports in real life but I enjoy this. The racquetball. I'm good. It's like grooves hang in the air of how I'm supposed to move and I just flow along them. My friend talks about a coworker of ours that annoys us. Then I talk to him about my fears. I feel like something icy has ungripped my heart. He understands me, he listens. This friend. He's like an amalgam of some real friends, and my dead dad, and a sitcom one. My muscles burn sweetly as I smash the ball.

Then I rush home to take a shower there. My house is like a combination of real houses I've owned but recast in a southern college town—maybe my idea of Savannah although I've never been. I have a front porch. I've never had a front porch in real life, always wanted one. With people walking along sidewalks and hanging outside of their front porches. I hear talk that this is a game night for this college town.

In my house there is so much space, ridiculous space. I check the answering machine—yes, an old school twentieth century answering machine. Tape. On it is my girlfriend asking about our dinner plans.

I get in the blue tiled shower with a small window up high bathing me in early evening blue. One thing these games really get right is light, and water. They've really figured out water. I've always loved showers; it's one of the closest things to weightlessness, to carefree bodilessness that one can achieve. You're thought-surfing on that calming whoosh of sound. But here it is different. I have a great body that just felt good, a body better honestly than any I ever had in real life, I'm bouncing on my toes with energy, and the hot water washing away my sweat just felt good and right.

But where are the ninjas, I wonder. I laugh. Maybe that was all a misdirect, the virt's sense of humor. Or maybe that is the name of a movie I will direct in this world. Maybe my first shot at directing will be a B movie, like a Roger Corman.

My eyes close and my mouth drinks in the hot, clean water. And almost on cue (no, exactly on cue—just like a movie) I hear the tiniest sound, a cloth shoe on tile, and then I felt a sharp blade against my throat. Then, a pause, *a comically timed pause, a professional television one-camera situation comedy pause,* and another blade presses against my reproductive organs. I open my eyes but my eyes are in the stream of the water. The faucets squeak as the water is turned off. And a voice, a young woman's, forceful: "Don't make a sound." I blink and the figure comes into focus.

Her face not far from mine, her big brown eyes stern, her pouty lips set in determination. She wears a mask that her black hair tumbles over, and a tight black outfit that I couldn't help notice didn't hide her, yes, big breasts that bobbed with slight animated exaggeration to her body movements like they were spring loaded, or animated by thirteen-year-old-boys. She pressed the blade against my neck harder, almost breaking skin.

"I am sorry to meet you like this," she says. "But we can't risk your escape. What we are about to tell you …"

"Are you sure?" asks a second, huskier voice behind me. Presumably she is the one brandishing the lower sword. "I don't think *he* can possibly be the one."

"There is no mistake."

"I am Belus. This is Tarpata. We are from Altair," says brown eyes. "The Varn have killed our people—the few of us left hide out on your planet."

"And why are you telling me this?"

"Because you are the one to lead us into victory to defeat the Varn. You are the one in the prophecy."

The prophecy? Really? That old story telling sawhorse?

I say, "Can I get a towel?"

Husky presses her lips into my ear and I can almost visualize her behind me, like this movie has suddenly gone from POV to a movie, and a cut of her lips whispering into my ear.

"Now he knows our names. If we can't train him we'll have to kill him. What if he's with the Varn?"

And suddenly it's all spinning like water down a drain and I'm back in my real apartment, back to my old self. Two hours have passed. My throat is parched. That went fast. I want to jump right back in, but I'm at my limit. Two hours tomorrow, after my great-great-grand's birthday.

Well, damn those programmers. Or the AI. I think they have it so it's programmed by AI anyway. I was skeptical but they've really got my number with that virt. What would the Varn be like? Bug-like? Or more of a secret agent green-skinned human kind of thing?

That little snippet even got me hard. Hard! I masturbate. In real life. It's been a while.

A memory from tenth grade. Me and Stephanie Berry dissecting the frog. She liked to bust my chops, and playfully threaten to stab my crotch with the x-acto knife. One time she misjudged and stuck me. I still have the tiny scar. She was mortified but I acted nonchalant. The truth was it drove me wild. Somehow the computer knew that and put a spin on it and used it on me.

I used to be in awe of my smallness in the universe. Now I'm in awe with my smallness in relation to technology. Double small.

WOLVERINES

My great-great-grand shows off his retractable claws. I stand in the corner. I'm not supposed to eat cake but I do it anyway. Sugar slows down the nanochondria that helps keep me alive. I'm 170 years old.

I think about Belus and Tarpata more. What will their training entail? I think about my lecture. Will fighting off the Varn mean a leave of absence, or can I somehow juggle it with my job in a sort of comic Peter Parker/Spider-Man sort of way?

CRACKITY

Back at the coffee shop. I see a man reading! SURRENDERS TO PLATO. It's a good novel. Eighty years old. "I remember when that was published. When that first came out. Good book," I say. He nods politely and turns subtly away from me. I tried.

I walk back to my apartment to get back to the virt. There are three figures on the stairs. One is genetically modified so his face looks reptilian. Another has extra arms—one cropping out of each shoulder like wings. I accidentally graze one. "Watch it," he says. Suddenly blackness.

OPTIONS

"Daddy's awake."

I wake up in a darkened room not my own. My daughters are there.

They're 140ish but they still call me Daddy.

I see the machines I'm plugged into. The hospital call button. The robonurse arms jut out from the wall above my head, dormant.

Britney looks like she has been crying. Justine says I fell down the stairs and broke my pelvis and spine.

She says I shouldn't have been walking the stairs alone at my age.

She says when I feel better, we need to discuss my options.

My options.

They can give me a new pelvis, but my legs are so brittle it would really entail a whole new skeletal system. There's a mechanically controlled exoskeleton with metal rods, but that's not comfortable. There's a hoverchair. There's a brain transplant, if I can find a suitable body donor. Also expensive. I could afford it but then I'd have no money to live on. And then of course there's the brainhousing.

They bring in a brainhousing salesman. He says that the brain is the most important part of the body anyway. Brains without bodies live longer. They are closely monitored. People on the outside can jack in and visit your world. My daughters could visit me. He gingerly floats out I could be with my loved ones again. The dead ones.

Britney says it sounds pretty good and maybe she should give it a try. Justine laughs nervously.

I start to drift off again and I hear my daughters talk as if I'm not there.

Justine says it's the most sensible thing. It's not about the money. It's not about saving money. It's what will allow me to live the longest.

Britney says it just feels weird. "It feels like he's dying. He won't be here anymore. He won't be here in a bed. There won't be anything here. We'll have to go into a virt to see him, and he'll probably be some young guy that doesn't even look like *Dad.*"

Justine says it's an adjustment. She feels the same way. But you have to do what's best. This is suffering. The thing is, she just wants to make sure I choose the right virtual. Something that will save my soul, and insure I go to heaven and not hell. One of the Mickey Jesus virts.

We can't rush him, Britney says.

Of course not. Let's talk with him about it when he gets out of the hospital.

Britney says if they're going to force me to ditch my body she's damn sure going to let me choose my own virtual.

The sisters agree. Once he gets out, we'll go on a picnic. At that place we used to go. We'll discuss the options.

MICKEY JESUS ASIDE

Mickey Jesus originated in Walt Disneyworld when a Mickey Mouse robot glitched and started spouting cryptic sentences. "The end time is a time of lights," etc. Mechanics took it in for repair only to find an oil stain in the shape of the Virgin Mary on its inner motors. The Mouse was bought by interested parties and became a prophet.

Mickey Jesus is now considered by two thirds of the world to be the second coming of Jesus. Mickey Jesus' beliefs center around wholesomeness, perkiness, cleanliness, and believing in yourself. Mickey Jesus sits at the third hand of God. Mickey Jesus virts, I suspect, probably have a lot of golf and soulless pop music with lyrics about the importance of a soul.

ROCK THE CASBAH

After two weeks, I am wheeled outside. There are other old people like me, ghosts haunted by their own dead pasts. I meet one who is humming a Clash song. "All Lost in the Supermarket." A band that used to be my favorite. I want to finish a lyric for him, but I can't remember it. So I just say, the Clash rocks! He smiles.

I look for him in his room the next day but it is empty. He has been brainhoused.

I jack in to pay him a little visit. He's playing guitar in a club in London. After the show I go backstage to congratulate him (for what? For his simulated guitar work?) but he is so surrounded by groupies our exchange is kept brief.

BY TWO POINTS

The Varn are invisible to human eyes. Belus has to open my eyes so I can see them. It happens in a magic sacred Altair ritual. Now I have an invisible third eye and the ability to run up walls.

On the way to racquetball, the Varn attack. I guess they've heard I'm prophesied to be their worst nightmare.

They're horrible blurred shadow things that seem to move at triple time. Four of them. But I'm prepared. Running up the wall I drop one with my racquet and another with a kick. I reach in another's chest and pull out its five chambered heart. Its soul flies screaming back to its home planet. Where's the fourth? Its claws are burrowing into my skull. Then a black figure—Tarpata—slices the Varn to oblivion. Her breasts graze my arms several times, gratuitously, as we flip about dispatching the several more that approach. She is pleased. "You're learning," she says.

I also win narrowly at racquetball.

HAVING ALL THE FUN

I usually hate picnics, but not this one. Justine, Britney, and the great-grands and the great-greats. We remember the good times. We eat mozzarella and tomato sandwiches on French bread—the tomatoes are fresh from my garden.

"I will visit you every week," says Britney.

Later, washing glasses, Justine makes an admission to Britney and me. "I'm getting brainhoused too," she says, a smile bursting out. "I'm one hundred-forty, Dad. And why should you have all the fun?" We all share a laugh not because it's funny exactly but it seems like the right reaction to put in the silent pause.

We finish and just take in the sun. Then, I stand up, wiping crumbs from my lap. My legs are so damn muscular I just bound up. I kiss them good-bye. Hug them. Always hug them like it might be the last time, because it might. They say they need to go. So do I—I have a lecture.

They turn to go their way, and disappear out of the virt. I run back to the faculty building. I turn invisible and scale a wall with terrifying stealth. Padding up the bricks, I wonder if Justine and Britney and the grandkids really jacked in and visited me in the virt, or if it is something the virt created because it knew it would make me happy. In the end, it may not matter. In terms of information received by my brain, there is effectively no difference.

On the roof I meet Belus and Tarpata. They have my next mission.

INTERMISSION

At the top of the sky scraper, the large breasted ninja jumps, plummeting faster and faster.

The ninja pulls off her mask, revealing a smirking Stiffany.

"Well, I hope you liked that story. To me it was sort of like 'The Matrix,' but without any action." She shrugs, then decapitates a window washer tied to his little platform as she continues to fall. Her body spins, allowing you to stare at it from several unusual and vaguely erotic angles.

"Our next story is about having a dream. Having ambition. I just hope things don't end badly." She points to the approaching sidewalk and upturned onlookers. "Like it is about to for these idiots!"

You turn the page before you hear the splat.

AN ASPIRING HABERDASHER

To: Honorable Mr. Hanso Keen, Assistant
Haberdasher (Wednesday) to the King
<hkeen@hisroyalnessinfiniteperfection.king>
From: x <X13294788@internetcafe.nil>

Dear Honorable Mr. Keen:

This is just a quick e-mail to say I am a fan of your haberdashery. I have always noticed the King's hats are especially fine on Wednesdays—there's something about the color palettes of the Wednesday hats in particular, they really bring out His Eyes, and the hats both manage to push the boundaries of exciting fashion while at the same time preserving the rich tradition of His Royal Personage; and they are always so well placed on His Highness's Head, at that perfect angle that is both imposing yet slightly roguish.

Imagine my surprise when I recently learned that my grandmother was once bathroom attendant to your Aunt F----- K------ in her summer estate in W-------.

It is my hope that I could repeat that pattern of my family working with yours. I would love to meet with you briefly to discuss if there are any entry-level positions in the field of Royal Haberdashery and perhaps show you my training in the choice and placement of hats upon heads through my portfolio or in person. I am known in my village for my ability to draw hats in the sand, and have even fashioned hats out of sticks and weeds. Crude imitations of the work you do, yes, but I hope it shows to you my desire to learn!

I currently live, as you can guess, in W------, about three days from the Capital by foot, so I would be available to see you as early as Wednesday.

Even if there are currently no positions available, I would still be most honored to meet you, if even for two minutes, but if you are not available I completely understand.

I thank you for taking the time to read this.

Humbly yet excitedly,
X

To: X13294788@internetcafe.nil
From: hkeen@hisroyalnessinfiniteperfection.king

Great memories of summers in W----- - badminton lemonade etc. There may be an opening. One of my assistant's ball-lickers took ill. A good mid-level gig as it allows you to be near my assistant and learn the ropes. More typical starting position is in stables licking asst asst asst haberdashers' horses' assholes and it's years before they get near actual asst asst asst haberdasher, let alone actual asst asst hab.

I should be on the Royal Promenade tonight sometime until 2am or so. Come out. Password to get by my guards is FUCKFACE.

To: hkeen@hisroyalnessinfiniteperfection.king
From: X13294788@internetcafe.nil

Dear Honorable Mr. Keen:

Thank you so much for the kind e-mail. Unfortunately I am three days away from the city, but I am going to run the entire time and try to make it in a day. Your kind words provide me the energy! Also, is there any particular area along the Royal Promenade I should look for you? It is my understanding from the maps on our village mural that the Promenade is thirty miles long and I would hate to wait for you in the wrong area.

Ready to run like the wind,
X

To: hkeen@hisroyalnessinfiniteperfection.king
From: X13294788@internetcafe.nil

Dear Honorable Mr. Keen:

I am happy to tell you I am breathing the refined air of the glorious Capitol City!

Unfortunately, even with my grandmother selling the tin from the roof of her hut to afford me passage by train, I was unable to arrive in the city until 3 a.m., one hour past your generous window.

Would it be possible to schedule another meeting? Name the time and place and I will be there. I have staked out an excellent area in the crowds just beside a bench offering a view of the Palace and also convenient to an Internet cafe. I will be checking my e-mail hourly at the cafe, or as close to hourly as possible as there are frequently long lines.

Very excited about the possibility of making the acquaintance of one of the haberdasher greats, as well as this potential job opportunity,
X

2 weeks later

To: hkeen@hisroyalnessinfiniteperfection.king
From: X13294788@internetcafe.nil

Dear Honorable Mr. Keen:

This is X, my grandmother was once bathroom attendant at your aunt's estate in W-------, and I had the honor of exchanging e-mails with you about the possibility of meeting you to discuss your amazing haberdashery as well a potential testicular licking opportunity.

I understand you are very busy but I just wanted to double check that you got my previous e-mails. You know how e-mail can be!

I believe I had the honor of witnessing you and your entourage take breakfast several times at the Diamond Cafe on your way to witness sport at the Royal Arena. Has a more formidable group of experts in the choice and placement of hats upon the Great One's head ever been assembled? Although my view was obscured by the hordes of onlookers gathered, a brief glimpse through two shoulders showed me that you are as handsome and intelligent as you are talented at haberdashery.

In conclusion, I would most enjoy a meeting at your earliest convenience. Also, unfortunately, I've been forced to reduce my e-mail checking to every two hours for budgetary reasons so my apologies in advance for any slight delay in my response.

Oh, and if you wish to speak to me at your breakfast, I would be most honored. I am in a white tunic and carrying a cardboard portfolio as well as a prototype hat made of leaves. To distinguish myself from all the others in similar circumstance, I will hold up three fingers to make a "W" in honor of the beloved village of your aunt's estate, W-------. I believe we are entering the rainy season there. My grandmother sent me word that, now without a roof, she finds the rains very refreshing and she sends you a thousand praises and thank yous for your kindnesses and generosities as well praise for your honorable aunt.

Faithfully yours,
X

2 weeks later

To: hkeen@hisroyalnessinfiniteperfection.king
From: X13294788@internetcafe.nil

Dear Honorable Mr. Keen:

It has occurred to me that I have possibly offended you in some way. In my earlier e-mail, I said, "You know how e-mail is!" I in no way meant that the Royal E-mail System was anything less than perfect, I was referring to the system at the Internet cafe.

Further, if there is anything I have done to offend you, I would like to humbly apologize and make it right. I would happily intern for free if you would give me the opportunity. I would gladly forego any salary, room or board forever for just an opportunity. The knowledge of being near great men who serve the king is all the salary I need, your mentorship better than any roof over my head, and all the sustenance I need can surely be found licking clean the assistant haberdasher's honorable scrotum.

Finally, and my apologies for this lengthy e-mail, I have had to reduce my e-mail checking to daily at 8 a.m. so I do apologize for that. Also, I had to sell my clothes so I will be standing in the pit cordoned off for the clothesless and the crippled, in the back alley behind the cafe near the bathrooms and balcony. I will be holding my cardboard portfolio to protect your eyes from my immodesty, and still holding up my hands to form a "W." Others in the crowd, jealous of my connection to you, have taken to imitating me and holding up their fingers in a "W" as well. To differentiate myself I will be alternately winking my left and right eyes and mouthing out the name of our beloved W-------.

Saddened by my transgressions and hopeful of your forgiveness,
X

To: X13294788@internetcafe.nil
From: hkeen@hisroyalnessinfiniteperfection.king

Heading to the beach sometime next week. Good time to meet up. Guard password I think is OLIVE TREE or maybe TREEHOUSE.

To: hkeen@hisroyalnessinfiniteperfection.king
From: X13294788@internetcafe.nil

Dear Honorable and Glorious Mr. Keen,

Oh, your e-mail, your glorious e-mail, is like milk to a newborn calf! So forceful! So direct and well worded! I am setting out to our glorious beaches immediately. Please sir, if you are able, could you kindly deign to tell me which beach? I have learned the most popular beaches for Royal Haberdashers are Jewel Beach and Crown Beach. I am walking (nay, running!) that way and will check e-mail as soon as I arrive.

Excitedly,
X

To: X13294788@internetcafe.nil
From: hkeen@hisroyalnessinfiniteperfection.king

Skiing at Majesty Mountain. Where r u?

To: hkeen@hisroyalnessinfiniteperfection.king
From: X13294788@internetcafe.nil

Dear Honorable and Compassionate Mr. Keen:

A thousand pardons, Mr. Keen. I misread your e-mail to say beach and I failed to ascertain you meant skiing. I can only imagine the pressures your lofty position subjects you to and completely understand how you must choose the most effective form of relaxation in the moment in order to insure optimum "recharging of the batteries" so to speak in order to best perform your numerous critical duties to the King.

Grandmother selling rest of house to afford passage to Majesty Mountain. Apologize in advance for my tardiness/nudity/filthiness/limp/sores.

With utmost hope and gratitude for your continued infinite understanding,
X

To: hkeen@hisroyalnessinfiniteperfection.king
From: X13294788@internetcafe.nil

Dear Honorable Mr. Keen:

Again a thousand pardons and apologies for our misunderstanding today, and my apologies for apologizing a lot

93

lately. I saw you and attempted to approach you with the passwords TREEHOUSE and OLIVE TREE and your guards understandably kicked me to the ground, kicking me about my face, body and genitals. I take full responsibility for this misunderstanding and for failing to confirm the passwords because I imagine you must change them frequently in accordance with security protocol of someone of your station. I did attempt to inform you that I was X, whose grandmother worked in the bathhouse of your aunt's summer estate in W------, etc., but you looked at me with understandable disgust and spat on me. I apologize that perhaps you did not recognize me. I regret I did drop my portfolio and leaf hat, and was unable to maintain making the "W" with my fingers due to unfortunate reflexive defensive gestures, and was likely unable to speak loudly enough for you to hear, my weakness/hunger/being beaten being no excuse.

On the other hand, if you did know it was me and merely decided I am not a "good fit" for your honorable organization, I do understand. I only await your judgment and will act accordingly.

Let me lastly say it has occurred to me that perhaps this altercation was indeed the interview. As my dry cracked tongue felt the wetness of its own blood and the hard sustenance of my own teeth, which I swallowed gleefully one by one like a fine feast, it occurred to me how much better one would be able to lick your assistant assistant's infinitely perfect gonads without teeth limiting movement or potentially causing harm to aforementioned tender part of honorable assistant assistant haberdasher.

Upon this realization as I lay on the ground being kicked, I tried to lick and caress each of my broken teeth to demonstrate and better train myself in the art of licking perfect, honorable testicles. In this context, your generous spit, which dropped into my mouth, was surely an act of mentorly kindness. You realized I was trying to demonstrate my abilities with a dry mouth, lacking adequate food and water these many months, and in your infinite wisdom you "lended a helping hand."

I only hope that I am worthy. Again thank you for your generosity and always being ten steps ahead and I thank you.

Lastly, please please know I am told my grandmother's final words were praise to your aunt and to you and your family, that she is so honored to have served your aunt and to have lived to see her son associate with a man as fine as you.

In Awe,
X

To: hkeen@hisroyalnessinfiniteperfection.king
From: X13294788@internetcafe.nil

Dear Mr. Keene,

Just a quick e-mail to say with great embarrassment that this will be my last e-mail as I am thoroughly out of funds. I will position myself as near to the "cripple pit" behind Diamond Cafe as possible. Unfortunately I will also be lying down, as one of my legs has decided to stop working. Darn legs! Nor do I trust my arms to hold up my fingers making the "W" sign so I have taken the liberty of carving a "W" with a piece of glass onto my belly, distended perfectly as if for this purpose.

In a fit of foolish hunger I ate my portfolio and leaf hat but have retained one scrap of paper, a drawing of a royal hat, that I will keep clutched in my left fist. On the off chance you come by and I am unconscious, I have procured a stick which you may use to awaken me.

If you see fit to meet with me, I will remain there faithfully at your service until death comes. If our paths do not cross again I can only hope my remains may somehow feed the cotton plants or the caterpillars spinning the silk that will go into the hats that the person you assist will one day place on the Great One's Head. My soul will do its utmost to reincarnate in a way useful to you as an assistant, or if that is too ambitious, a caterpillar or perhaps even a bacterium breaking down the feces inside someone moderately close to you.

Forever in your debt,
X

i am lying in the street in my diarrhea it is a dark moonless night and I cant see but I suspect it is blood and diarrhea I cannot help it but I imagine licking your balls and then biting them off and turning them into my diarrhea going diarrhea on all your hats and I laugh and laugh you are angry and then the diarrhea is on you and you are melting into the diarrhea until I am choked with laughter and dry tears on my cheeks the diarrhea floods the world melting it and you and the guards and the crowds and the king are all melted into my diarrhea until it is only me swimming in it and my body wracks with laughter, choking in it

INTERMISSION

On the small table is a fruity drink, ice melting rapidly, with festive miniature umbrella. Beside it, also on the rim of the volcano, is an orange beach recliner. On the recliner lies Stiffany. She wears a bikini—black with little skulls.

"Like what you see?"

The detective looks to the policemen with disdain.

"Don't get cute," he replies. "Cause of death?"

They stand over Stiffany. Her skin paler than even before. Her eyes dead still, staring off into nothing.

"Unclear," says the policeman. "We were going to take her to autopsy after we finished up with the photos. One suspicion is that her sun screen," he holds up a plastic bag inside of which is a bottle of sun screen labeled "SUN SCREAM," "may have been poisoned. But who knows with these things? The literary horror host types have their own unique body chemistry."

"Any possible suspects?"

"Well, she'd just gotten a job hosting a short story collection and the previous host was disgruntled. He'd been fired. But also she's got a long list of ex-lovers. And just in the course of her job as a horror character she's killed, or done horrible things to, any number of people, drank wine out of a pizza delivery guy's skull and all that. Just killed a window washer yesterday. And some bystanders. So it could have been one of those family members. And apparently she was blackmailing her bosses with compromising photos."

"Dust for prints." The detective wipes his sleeve on his forehead. "Jesus, it's hot."

"It's a fucking volcano, boss."

"Yeah."

A policeman zips the body bag.

"Stiffany's got it 'in the bag.' Ha ha hooowwwl!"

The detective turns to see, off to the side of the squad car, a werewolf in a red and orange fast food costume. On his breast pocket is stitched the logo WOLF IT DOWN BURGERS.

"How about that last story, folks? Hats off to that one! Haw haw howl!" he says. "Allow me to introduce myself. I'm your new host, 'Fur'-geson the Fast Food Werewolf, where we provide the fast and you provide the food. Ha ha hoow—"

"Please," says the detective. "This is a crime scene. Keep it behind the yellow tape."

"Fur"-geson moves quickly, on all fours, head butting the detective into the volcano so fast he doesn't even have a chance to scream.

The policeman reaches for his gun but before he can fire the werewolf is behind him.

"Next up, a tale about desire called Sex Fantasies at Work! But watch out for that *twist*," he says, twisting the cop's neck, causing it to snap loudly followed by several smaller pops, like knuckle cracks, "ending! Ha ha hooowwwl!"

He pauses for a moment, holding the cop still for effect. Maybe he's hoping you'll take a picture for reference for a book cover.

After he thinks you're gone, he walks down the volcano to his car, an '09 Scion. He takes out his cell and calls his girlfriend.

"Hey baby," she says.

"Hey. Sorry I didn't call you sooner. I was hosting a short story."

"I know. I was calling you to check on you. How did it go?"

"Well, I think ... I don't know. I tried to keep it short and sweet. Not overstay my welcome. And we tried to incorporate Stiffany's death in an interesting way, but tasteful."

"I bet you were great. I can't wait to see it. I'm soooo proud of you, honey."

"Yeah, I'm excited. I just—I just wish it had happened under different circumstances. With Badbones getting fired. And Stiffany dead. I mean, they are giants in the industry. And I don't want a perception that I'm happy about what happened to them, or that I'm some scab host, or that I'm climbing over a bunch of corpses to get here. I was asked to take over this franchise and I was excited to do it."

"I'm sure nobody will think that about you, honey. I wouldn't worry."

"I just don't want to get a rep as the backup host. The third pick. I am my own host."

"I wouldn't worry about that. I mean, how many people will make it this far in the book anyway?"

"What? What is that you said?"

"Nothing. I'm—I'm sure it will be great."

"You said nobody is going to read my part of the book?"

"That's not what I said. I just said, it's not like this book is being published by a big house with a bunch of PR, so you're allowed to mess up a little."

"What kind of backhanded bullshit is this? You think I'm messing up? You don't think this is a big break?"

"My words are coming out wrong, honey. I have a headache. Can't we discuss—can't we talk about this later?"

"You said nobody is going to read this book. And I'm messing up."

"That's not what I meant, baby. I'm sorry. I'm sorry."

"I gotta go."

"Are you still mad?"

"I gotta go."

"You are mad. I'm sorry. I'm stupid."

"I gotta go. The police are starting to show up."

"Fur"-geson hangs up. He scratches his jaw.

The phone rings again. It's from his girlfriend but he doesn't answer it.

He takes a large plastic WOLF IT DOWN cup of soda out of the car and takes a drag on the straw. The drink is warm and watery.

SEX FANTASIES AT WORK

1.

I feel like I'm always at work.

I'm not saying I work too much. I put in forty-five hours a week, if that.

Nor am I saying that I take work home with me, either, or that I can't shift mental gears to my personal time.

I am saying it literally feels like I'm always in this cube, in my grey chair, gaining weight, armrests cutting in my thighs, khakis cutting into my gut (need to go up a size), always staring at the screen, managing the medical databases, always walking through the hall to get coffee, or raid the candy dish, or steal a glance at Amber, always lifting my glasses and rubbing my palms in my eyes.

I know I'm not making sense.

I go home every night, obviously. I have friends outside, and hobbies, and interests, etc. But it's like I don't really live them out; they're, like, wispy or something. It's like they're just memories that are implanted in me. It's like I'm a robot that is just programmed to think it has a home life, but that really just works all the time.

But of course that makes no sense. If I was a robot why the need for a fake home life at all? And why bother making me fat, or adding all these weird specific details of my life, or why bother making me human at all? Plus, if I was a robot, surely they would program me to work harder than I actually do.

I bet you work harder than you realize.

If you grade on a curve I do. More than most of the schmucks in the place. But since I'm pretty good at what I do and nobody really understands it or wants to, and since so much of the work is autopilot stuff, really, really repetitive stuff, it affords me a ton of time to think.

What do you think about? While you're feeling always at work?

Primarily I daydream. And primarily those daydreams involve sex.

Tell me one.

2.

I am in my apartment. It's 3 a.m. I can't sleep. I'm too tired to care about the Internet, or watching TV, or playing a computer game, or reading one of the seven books on my night stand, face down, open to where I stopped reading like a little array of pitched roofs, a tiny village of attention deficit disorder. I'm just in a tired, angsty fog. I know something is fucked about my life; somewhere, people who have their shit together are living my wildest dreams. I need to "pick myself up by my bootstraps" and "take some initiative" and "believe in myself" and "prioritize goals" and all that crap, but I'm just too tired, too foggy to care.

That's when I hear that thump on the roof. It sends a shot of adrenaline in me. I've woken up before with a vague feeling that there had just been a sound on the roof, but this is the first time

I'd heard it awake. What could it be? I'm on the top floor of our apartment building. Is it kids fucking around? I throw on some shorts and sandals and head into the hallway.

Sliding the big, rusty door to the roof stairway slowly and quietly, I feel my way up the dark stairs. The door on the roof is ajar; I crouch in the shadows and peek out.

The figure is crouched on the edge of the roof. My eyes adjust to the darkness and the details begin to fill in. I see the graceful silhouette of a woman. A beautiful woman. She wears boots, hot pants, and a tiny cape, a decorative cape that doesn't even reach her exposed midriff. The slightest curve of baby fat circling her waistband. I admire the tautness of her lower back, and her ass. She's squatting on the end of the roof, still, looking out, contemplating.

It dawns on with a shock that this is Mistress Medic. The white blonde hair. The shape of the nurse themed hat that I knew had MM emblazoned on it. She speaks.

"The city."

I freeze. Does she sense me? No. She is talking to herself. Proclaiming something. A private monologue.

"The city is an open wound. The city is a cry of pain. I must heal it!"

And with that she inhales, tenses her thighs, and jumps out like a shot into the darkness, ten stories up, gliding and jumping from building to building using her Lariat of Healing and the proprietary adhesive strips on her hands and feet.

I know that superheroes like to have a perch, somewhere they like to sit and contemplate dramatic things before they go off to nab a bank robber or battle Dr. Disastro. And apparently Mistress Medic occasionally uses my roof! Mistress Medic, one of the League of Invincibles, standing a mere fifteen feet above my bed! Probably more than once. Is it possible her secret identity lives in my building? My brain scans through the tenants—there are some young women in my building but their bodies didn't match up. Either too heavy, too skinny, too slouchy, breasts not big enough. No hiding MM's breasts. They're even better than Amber's, at work, when she wears that little cardigan and the too low shirt.

I'd seen MM on the news, looked at pictures of her on the web—yes, I admit it—pictures snapped by pervs like me from all different angles on HeroVoyeur.com. A nice ass shot while she's fighting Fin Fatale, a nip slip while she saves a burn victim. Mistress Medic, with her big innocent blue eyes, her full lips, her willowy tall yet surprisingly muscular body. She doesn't seem like she's even of this Earth. She's just perfect from every angle, and every pose, gravity defying, like God was a comic book artist and just constructed her to be the perfect male fantasy.

I go back down to my apartment absolutely shaking with adrenaline. How many times had I dreamed of meeting her? Or the others?

All across the city, beautiful young men and women were fighting crime. But I was less concerned about the men. It was the women. Impossibly strong, impossibly beautiful women, young, some wearing spandex, some basically glorified bikinis, with boots—oh the boots!—going out doing good. The devilish Roaring Rogue with the fishnets. Megaton Maiden—with the strength of a thousand suns and hips to match. Many times I daydreamed of robbing a bank just to get picked up by one of them. Oh, just to have the gloved perfect hand of Purple Passion touch my face, even if it was in a punch. And now I had had one on my roof. Mistress Medic. The sweetest and cutest one of the bunch.

Mistress Medic. Some says she's an alien, others a fallen angel, others say she was bombarded with radiation during an experimental medical procedure. The point is, her hands can heal anything—a broken neck, a severed head—anything short of absolute death. And an idea forms in my head.

The next time she appears on my roof, I'll be ready. I'll buy a gun, and when she appears, I'll shoot my abdomen. I'll stumble up to the roof. "I've been shot!" I'll fall to the ground, moaning.

She'll run to me, her sweet, concerned face hovering over me. I'll swim in those big blue concerned eyes of hers.

She'll lift up my shirt and lay her hands on my stomach, on the wound. No, I have a fat, unflattering stomach and the jiggling will kill the mood. I'll shoot myself in the shoulder. She'll lay her hand on my shoulder and the magic healing will begin. Will it hurt? Is it hot? Cold? Electrical? Does it simply feel like a pretty girl's hand on me? I'll have some lines prepared. I'll be grateful, but humorous about it. "What's a nice super heroine like you doing on a crappy roof like this?" or, no, something simple, like, "It just went from the worst day of my life to the best."

I'll heal up but she'll insist on taking me to the hospital for further tests. She always does that, maybe it's a lawsuit thing. She'll pick me up in her arms—so strong, strong enough to break brick walls, yet still so impossible rounded and soft. My torso pressed up against her breasts, mashing her breasts, housed in the thinnest of superhero fabric, and low cut with the "MM" logo over the left nipple. I'll look down at her breasts. She'll notice. I'll say "You've changed your insignia, haven't you?" She'll nod, talking about branding, and how hard it is to be a superhero and not seem ridiculous. I'll point out how much I admire that she is a superhero at all. I'll say, "You'd think a person of your powers would just open up a medical practice and heal people all day, and get rich, but here you are going out into danger, saving lives." She'll say something like she likes the adventure, needs it, and I'll say I admire that, I envy it, even, with my routine life, and our eyes will lock in a funny way, like we're about to kiss, and I'll lean in to do it, but stop, laughing nervously at my boldness, and apologizing, and she'll say "No, it's okay," and I will kiss her, just a brief one at first, and pull back and make a joke about her swinging through the buildings with her eyes closed and even if she accidentally smacked into a building it would be worth it. No, too fawning. Keep it casual. I won't say anything. And then we'll go find the top of another roof and make out. Just full on neck for maybe twenty minutes to an hour.

We'll reach the hospital and before I check in I'll ask for a way to contact her.

And she'll say no. Surely she'll say no. And we wouldn't have made out. I wouldn't have kissed her at all, nor would our eyes have locked in a way like she wanted me to kiss her, because she didn't want me to kiss her. Surely guys hit on her all the time, right? Guys way better than me? Aren't I a fool to assume we'd click? Who cares? I'd still get to spend some time with her. That's the most one can ask for, right?

After spending far too long looking at pictures of her on the Internet, and dreaming of us being a couple—a couple!—I flop on my bed. Now I really can't sleep. Adrenaline. I'll go and buy a gun tomorrow. I'll scan news sites to track her movements and whereabouts. If she's in Russia fighting the mob with the League of Invincibles, obviously I can take a break. I need to maximize my chances of being awake next time she's on my building, and maximize my sleep otherwise.

Should I set up a camera? A wireless motion detector? Surely a superhero as great as her is hyper-observant, trained to notice the unusual. Her life depends on it. Which begs the question, why didn't she hear me coming up the stairs? Maybe she did? What if she lives somewhere around here. Maybe she's seen me. She perched on the roof hoping I'd come up? No. Stupid, stupid fantasy. Superheroines date Superheroes. Guys who can fly them, who can leap buildings with them. Or at least rock stars or billionaire industrialists. But I do know that Mistress Medic has been hurt by those guys. She's had rocky relationships. Dudes who take her for granted and cheat on her. Maybe she's ready to take a try on a guy like me?

Maybe we do hit it off. We start dating. Maybe I convince her that the superhero life is too dangerous. I love her too much. Instead she could just use her powers to save lives all day. People could line up. I'd run the front desk. We'd marry. She'd wear her old Mistress Medic sometimes just for me in bed. I could just scoop my hands into that v-neck and let her out ...

My fully realized daydream evaporates with the sound of another thump. The hairs on my neck stand out like my own Spidey sense. Is she already back? I can't believe my luck. Can I really be sure she'll ever come back again? I must act now.

No time to buy a gun. Grabbing a kitchen knife, I pad back to the hallway and up the stairs as quickly and quietly as I can. I'm in underwear and a T-shirt. My heart is just pounding like a series of hand grenades being set off. I can't believe it isn't heard throughout the city. I'm gasping for breath but I hold it, hold it, I have to slow down. Can't scare her.

I peek through the sliver of the door. There she is. How can my desire for her at once be so base and so adoring? I want her tits. Her ankles. Her knees. I want her ass in that little blue hot pants number that she calls a superhero outfit. She's dressing like she wants it. Showing all that luscious leg. I want to see the fine blonde hairs on her leg. But at the same time I want to care for her. I want to pet her like a small bird. I want to protect her from harm. I want to fuck her blind. I want to just sit on a porch swing with her, the sound of cicadas, we're splitting a bottle of Spanish red wine. I want to just kiss her eyelids and talk all night, enjoying her company and my own frustrated erection. I want to come on her back. I want to pick up her dry cleaning. I want. I want.

She's perched there like a butterfly. Like a magic bird. One small misstep and she's going to fly. I need to act now. I hold the knife to my shoulder. There's some part of my brain that kicks in —holds my hand back. "Fuck you, you're not doing that," it says.

She examines her sleeve. "Dammit. Another bullet hole. Another uniform shot! They don't tell you about that in superhero school."

Her legs tense, she's about to leap. I've got no time—no time no time!

"Help!" I yell, faux weakly. And without thinking I plunge the knife—not into shoulder, but into crotch—slicing along my dick and cutting right through my balls.

Somehow, in the panic of the moment, part of my brain thought if I stab my dick she'll at least have to touch it to heal it —the worse I cut my balls the longer she'll have to cup them. We could have a conversation while she cups my balls. And surely that might lead to sex? Even if it doesn't, I still had Mistress Medic grab my junk. And not through clothes but skin on skin. I will always have that. She may never love me. She may never kiss me, or even remember I exist, but she will always have held my dick and balls for a little while. I can die having that.

It hurts like hell and then it doesn't. The adrenaline is kicking in.

"Help!" I yell again. The knife clatters down the stairs. She turns.

I go up the stairs and fall to the floor. The blood is running down my legs. There's a flap of underwear open, maybe I can see one of my balls coming out of the scrotum. Hard to tell with all the blood. I can't look or I'll faint.

She turns and runs to me. She leans over me, her hair hanging down loosely around her face. Her eyes of thoughtful concern. For the first time I'm close enough to notice her eyebrows, fine white hairs that blend in with her skin at a distance. Her hand presses down on my thigh. Assessing the damage. "What happened?" she asks.

"Some ... crazy guy stabbed me," I say. I try to add a note of fear in there. Which isn't even acted. I've really fucked my balls up. Is there a limit to how much she can heal them?

She stands up. "You're going to be okay. Hold on. Did you see where he ran off to?"

"Down the ... stairs."

She gets up. "Describe him. Was it just one?"

"I ... didn't get a good look. Feeling ... dizzy ..."

"I'm going to take a look ..."

She starts pulling down my underwear. She looks calmly, but I detect a slight wince. I look down, but she pushes my head down.

"Describe who stabbed you."

I'm definitely not going to say someone black. Or homeless. They get shafted enough already. "A white guy. In a suit. Seemed well to do. He just seemed like he ... he ... had a crazy glint in his eye. Maybe some coked up lawyer. Red hair."

"Well, he got you good here. But have no fear. I'm Mistress Medic. I'm going to heal the area here. And to do that, I'm going to have to touch the area."

"Okay," I say.

She puts her hand down and she's holding me in her hands. She's doing it.

"It's going to burn a bit."

"Okay," I say.

"I usually don't allow this until—" I start to joke. But then I feel the rays.

"Aigh," I say.

It's completely non sexual. It's totally not hard, and withdrawn in my body. Tiny, bloody thing. How did I think this was a good idea?

"I usually don't allow this until a second date," I say.

She lets out a funny sound. Not a laugh, but not not a laugh. Maybe it's the universal sound for acknowledging a joke has been told.

She brings her wrist bracelet to her lips. She talks to some sort of cell phone device in there. "Stabbing at 357 on 10th. Assailant: Caucasian, red hair, suit. Probably has some blood on his sleeve."

I have a great view up her skirt as she squats next to me, her superhero panties. But I try not to leer. I look in her eyes, and try to be professional, and sort of hoping she will look into my eyes and they will lock. But she's looking around, at the wound, at the sky, back at her wrist communicator, whispering information. I try to enjoy her hand on my groin despite the burning. But by the time I calm down enough to really think about it, she's done.

Should I try to repeat my joke about the second date?

"You're healing up there." She pulls out some antiseptic wipes and cleans off her hands. "But I'll take you to the hospital just the same. First, let me investigate where you were stabbed."

"On the stairs … on the stairs there."

She goes over the door and enters the stairwell. I'm laying on the ground with my underwear still down, feeling like an idiot. I'm just another victim to her. One of many. Like a stripper and her million customers. I have to think of something to help me poke through.

I sit up and look at my crotch. The cuts are gone but it's still bloodcaked, hairy, pale. Blood on my underwear. Am I really going to ask her out like this?

She returns holding the knife in a baggy. "I think I have prints," she says. "We'll get the perp. You can pull up your underwear."

I get up and pull up my underwear. I feel stupid.

"I'm going to call you an ambulance."

"Oh? I thought …"

"What?"

"I just thought … you said you were going to take me to the hospital, is all."

"I'm going to hunt down whatever sicko did this to you."

"I don't know. If it's okay … if it's okay for you to take me to the hospital … That guy is probably long gone."

"You don't even really need to go to the hospital. Just keep some ice on it to keep down the swelling. Sometimes my powers can't heal nerve endings. You may find a loss of sensation."

"Sensational," I say. Which is a terrible joke, and makes me seem like I'm ungrateful. What a stupid thing to say.

"You really have this case by the balls," I say. I'm blowing this. What the fuck am I doing?

"But seriously. Thank you. I've been a fan of yours for a long time and I just—"

"There's no need—"

"But seriously. Of all the superheroes, you are by far the best. I mean—"

"Thank you. Do you live near here?"

"Yes, just down stairs, actually. You can—"

"Why don't you go downstairs and get some ice. I think you can just go to the hospital in the morning."

"Oh, shit. You know what? I just remember him saying something. Dipping that knife in some toxin or something. Like he was part of Purple Poisoner's gang."

"What?" she asks. "Why didn't you say that before?"

"I'm sorry. I—I'm not myself—"

She looks at me skeptically. "Okay, let me take you."

When was the last time I was picked up by a woman? Seven? But I can't say it's unpleasant at all. It's kind of awesome.

She's swinging us through the city. My arm is around her shoulder—her hair flitting around on my elbow. Her breasts jutting into my side. She looks straight ahead.

"I'll rush that knife to the lab to identify any toxins. And the fingerprints."

"Hopefully the prints aren't just mine. I pulled the knife out. Just reflex, you know."

"We'll see."

"Thanks again. You really are great," I say.

She doesn't seem to respond to compliments at all. What else have I got?

"It must be tough being a superhero. It must really screw with your social life."

"A little bit," she says.

"Are most of the people you save grateful, or are some real dicks?"

"Most are grateful."

"That's good," I say.

How long does it take to swing to the hospital? I probably don't have much more time. I keep looking at her eyes but she keeps looking straight ahead.

"Is there a way I can repay you? Can I take you to dinner?"

She laughs. "That's quite alright."

"I insist. You saved me."

"I never fraternize with the people I save."

I'm running out of options. This is a game that can't be won. She just isn't interested in me. I suppose I should just go for broke. Before I can even think about it, the words are coming out.

"Listen, I have to tell you something. It's going to sound stalker-y but I'm not stalker-y. It's just, I've admired you from afar for years. I've had a crush on you. I know you've had boyfriends that don't understand you. They don't respect you. I had to meet you. You have to understand. I—I stabbed myself to meet you."

"I know," she says. "I know that wound was self-inflicted. I've been in this business long enough to know wounds."

"So you knew," I said. "But still you saved me."

"I'm not taking you to the hospital," she says.

"You're not?" A shot of excitement fires through me. Some naive, love struck part of my brain thinks: She's taking me to her apartment! She's lonely too. She's found someone she can connect with! She's ...

She lets go. I try to grab her hair but she swats me away. There's fury on her face. Such hate. I look at her pleadingly. As if to say, "But you're one of the good guys. How could you do this?"

And I'm falling, falling. And I think I must have triggered a lot of hate there. Or maybe she has this dark streak that is kept hidden. She sure hates me. Looking down I see the smoke stack I am falling into. Wondering if the heat will kill me, or the fall, or will the fear of this kill me first?

3.

At what point do you ejaculate? When you're falling down the smoke stack?

What? I'm not masturbating. I'm just sitting at my desk.

After hours?

I'm not masturbating. I'm just thinking.

Are you aroused?

Sometimes. It presses up against my desk, which gets me more aroused. I can tap out a little Morse code with my erection. I can't believe I'm talking about this. But that's not the point. The point is I'm always thinking about this stuff. I live in a soup of these daydreams.

Does it arouse you when the Medical Superhero—

Mistress Medic. But the name changes. Night Nurse. Crimson Cleric.

Does it arouse you when she drops you down the chimney? Are you into humiliation, failure?

No! I wish I was. I would love it if I was turned on by humiliation and failure. My life would be a nonstop orgy. No, I'm not turned on by that. I don't think. But then, you're the expert.

What part does turn you on?

Thinking about how she looks. The part where I think my plan might work. The part where she's touching me.

What would happen you if she's touching you, healing you, as you say, and then she looks you in the eye and says "Hey, I like you. Would you like to have a cup of coffee?"

That's not realistic.

But it's a daydream. And she's a superhero! That's not realistic.

True. But if superheroes *were* real, they would be like celebrities, and there would be a ton of schmoe guys like me mooning over the female superheroes. And I wouldn't stick out as anything special. I just wouldn't. Just because it is a daydream, and there are some fantastical elements, doesn't mean you can throw all logic out of the window.

What if you were the superhero, saving her? And you were very muscular, attractive, and all that?

My power of imagination is not that strong.

Do you ever have thoughts of harming yourself? I have to ask.

4.
(Something He is Too Embarrassed to Even Tell Dr. Ash)

When I was a little kid I used to think life was sort of fair. Like, if you're good looking, you're probably dumb. If you're ugly, you're smart, or maybe rich. If you're rich and pretty, you are probably shallow and thus unable to enjoy life. If you are poor and ugly, you are probably wise, or spiritually deep. I thought everyone was born with a gift, a purpose.

By the time I got to college I realized this wasn't true at all. I came to realize that my "gift," intelligence, wasn't even that special. I was just smart for my high school. My class had beautiful, rich people who were way smarter than me. And kinder, more generous. More talented. More ambitious. My dreams of secret greatness were illusions. There were people who were just so much better than me in every way, I couldn't even be jealous of them. I could only marvel.

So I developed a habit. If the world was full of smart, beautiful, women way out of my league, why not try to be around them as much as I could? I researched photos on the web to find a primary care physician who was beautiful. I did that with all services I needed. I have a cute dentist, a moody but gorgeous hair stylist, a really fuckable optometrist, a hot accountant. I did this to try to train myself to be more comfortable around women, especially pretty ones, in situations where they weren't allowed to openly loathe me. And that's how I picked you as a therapist, Dr. Ash. I got a list of therapists in my area and then searched a lot of images on the web. You were my favorite.

I was worried it might limit what I said to you, like a small part of me would think I had a chance to have sex with you so I needed to impress you and therefore hold back on my deep, dark shit. But that hasn't really happened. I so badly needed to unload my deep dark shit, I just let it out on you. To smart, beautiful you, Dr. Ash. When I talk, I look at the reflection of your legs in the window. You are so much younger than me but so much smarter. You look smart in that dress. I love your serious eyes, Dr. Ash.

I wish I was more mature. I wish I didn't think about tits so much, for example. Nobody wakes up in the morning and says "I want to be creepy." It's just what I am. Dr. Ash, your boobs wear a spiderweb bra and my eyes are flies.

5.

Today I want to get away from superheroes and such, a little, and get a little closer to your life. I want you to tell me about Amber, this girl at work you've mentioned. Do you have fantasies about her?

All the time.

6.

It started innocently. A cough. A slight fever. Itchy throat. But then, within twelve hours, death. It was extremely contagious. Before the world even had time to react the damage was done. But here was the thing. It only affected men. Young, old, male fetuses still in the womb even, it didn't matter. But it only killed men.

I'm not sure why I even bothered, but when it all went down I actually tried to call in sick to work (nobody answered). Then I just holed up in my apartment, debating whether I should put sheets over the air vents, waiting to die.

I lived on macaroni and cheese, peanut butter, peeks out the window to the parking lot below, and increasingly horrifying news on the Internet. E-mails from friends about who else was dead. E-mail chains with desperate theories on how not to get sick. Vitamin C. Estrogen hormones. Self castration. Etc. News that even the sperm in sperm banks was dying.

Mom sent me one about how man had sinned and this was God's punishment, but she added since I was not a sinner I should be okay but I should pray for forgiveness just in case. I just let that one go.

America and Europe were in a bad way. Other parts of the world like the Middle East, parts where women traditionally were less equal, were presumably even worse. It was hard to tell because they were without power and in total communications darkness.

Every few days my mom dropped off groceries and I told her I loved her through the door. She included antiseptic wipes I would use to wipe down every box before I opened it. She would say who had died. She would say how some things weren't available, like milk. Then for a while, nothing was available.

I thought about the men in my life. My father had died when I was ten, and I didn't have brothers. But I thought of my friends from school. I thought of my friends from work. Gary.

Dave. No more lunches at Bennigan's, while they talked about football and I pretended to be interested.

Then the Internet went down, followed by the power going out and Mom didn't come by. Weeks went by like this. I was resorting to my lesser canned goods, the things I might donate for a food drive—creamed corn, apple pie filling, two bites allowed per meal. Out the window, women dragged bodies and left them on the tennis courts over by parking lot. Grieving, shell-shocked women. That girl Sasha down the hall who I had had a brief conversation by the mailboxes about the French New Wave was there. She was in track shorts and a hoodie and running shoes, crying and dragging her roommate Derik down to the tennis courts. She had dancer's legs. There were some other girls there I'd seen around. Not too many. I guess a lot had gone to be with their families. I had a flash fantasy of just walking down the steps totally nude, swinging a big erection. Or lifting up the window blinds to reveal my naked self. "Hey everybody, I'm a guy and I'm alive! Fuck me!" But then I saw a mom and a little girl down there. They were carrying a big body wrapped up in a sheet. The husband. And then another wrapped sheet. A little one.

After some time the power came back on. And then the Internet. I charged my cell phone. A female president and vice president had been sworn in. They were putting the toll at 160 million dead in America alone. The president said the focus, beyond finding a cure, was burying the bodies and distributing food and water. Helping the elderly and children. Looking for surviving men, any men, but there were none so far. Maybe they were in hiding like me. Thirty-five Russian men had recently emerged from a submarine to much fanfare. Handsome young men in their twenties, with military chests. Despite transporting them in special sterilized trucks to a germ free holding lab, they all died. That really broke the hearts of the world. A hastily assembled military started to make the rounds, keeping order. But there weren't any riots. Crime was insanely low.

Every time I sneezed my heart would start pounding with panic that this was the beginning of the end. I would berate myself for not doing something more with what life was left.

Finally, I screwed up the courage to call Amber from work to mention I was still alive.

"Hello?"

"Hey, Amber." My voice felt weird and slurry because it had been so long since I had spoken.

"What? Who is this?"

"Clay."

"Clay?!!"

"From the office."

"I know from the office. You're ..."

She was silent.

"Yeah, I'm alive. Knock on wood. Ha ha. Where are you? Are you at work?"

"What? No, no. There's no work anymore, Clay. People don't need medical databases right now." Another pause. "Where are you?"

"At my apartment. Holing up here."

"Huh. That's amazing. Wow."

"Hey, listen, Amber, I was wondering if I could see you."

"What?"

"I don't know. Maybe hang out and watch a movie."

"Watch a movie? What are you talking about?"

"I don't know. We don't have to watch a movie."

"It's the end of the world."

"I know. I know. It's just ... I thought we always had fun talking at work. I thought we could get together."

She exhales and it's amplified in Clay's ear.

"I'm up at my parents' house. In Boston."

"What is that? Five hours?"

"Give or take."

"Well, what do you say? Can you come down?"

"I don't know. This is just sudden. I don't even know if

they're letting people on the freeways, Clay."

"I read that the roads are clear as of this week. I could come see you. We could meet somewhere in the middle."

"I don't know, Clay. I've … I've had to bury my dad and my brothers. I can't go through this again."

"It's okay. I don't have any symptoms yet."

"I might get you infected."

"I miss you."

"You barely know me. We were acquaintances at work."

"This is me wanting to get to know you. It's not like you have a job. What have you got to lose? Take a chance!"

"I don't know. I have a lot going on here. With my mom. She's a wreck."

"I could come up."

"I'm sure you there's a bunch of people in your area—"

"Amber. This might be your last time talking to a man ever. You might be talking to the last man on earth. This is my dying wish to see you, Amber. This is my dying wish."

"I can't do this, Clay. I have to go."

"Seriously? You're hanging up with the last man on earth?" I started to get mad. "I mean, maybe I'm not awesome but I'm okay. I'm okay! And what if I have some immunity? I'm going to have to repopulate the planet by myself. I mean, they're going to have to ration my semen. This is your chance to get in on the ground floor."

"I need to go."

"Amber, it's the pie filling. I've been surviving on pie filling and I'm light headed—"

Even as the possible last man on earth I was fucking things up. The phone rang again and for the tiniest instant I thought it was Amber calling to apologize. But caller ID said it was Mom. I let it go to voice mail. Then I decided I'd better call her back or she'd freak out thinking I was dead.

Not much to do but pace and replay the debacle with Amber in my head. My thoughts were utterly spirit destroying. I felt like the mental version of a cutter—those morose teenage girls that get pleasure from slicing their own skin. This was not good. I needed to get out of this rut. I needed to take the heat of rejection and self loathing and channel it outward into bold action. I needed to keep moving forward, keep running into the fire, keep asking women out. Just keep doing it and keep doing it until it worked and whatever desperate stink I had on my soul was cleansed once and for all. A plan started to form where I would walk over to Sasha's. This time I would act differently. I would be sad and say my dad had just died. Maybe I would act scared that I was going to die, too. The truth was I was scared I was going to die, but somehow I felt if I had to act it, it would come off phony. Fuck it, I said to myself. You're over thinking, I said to myself. I decided I was going to walk over to Sasha's and just be my honest self. I was just going to go and be myself and if she finds that repulsive too, fine, at least I tried.

As I was getting ready the phone rang again. Again a sliver of hope it was Amber. And this time, it was.

"Hey," she said. "I was thinking about our call ..."

She was different. More contrite. And was it? Yes, more flirty. She said she'd reconsidered and wanted to visit! She said her mom had insisted on it. She wanted to drive down with her sister! The thought of a three-way appeared and was repressed. She said she would be there tomorrow.

That's the way it is in life, I thought. You just need to try. Right? I thought I had been turned down, but I hadn't given up, I had pressed on with this plan to go see Sasha, and the universe had somehow picked up on this and gave me a break with Amber.

The temptation might have been to kick back, but I was determined to capitalize on this momentum and go see Sasha immediately. You see, Sasha had that whole runner, dancer body. And Amber had more of that cute baby fat, big boobs thing. Other guys had had sex with different women in a twenty-four-hour period. Here was my chance to "catch up." Should I take a shower? No, it will add to the desperate/about to die/end of the world vibe if I'm a bit sweaty and unkempt. "End of the world" vibe? Why are my own thoughts so weird? Are other people this terrible? Half the world is dead. My entire gender is dead or almost dead and I'm trying to affect an "end of the world" vibe. Maybe with a little gel in the hair. Oh, stop! Just be yourself. Just be your fucking self. But what if this sort of horrible, over thinking, conflicted thing **is** myself? Well, just stop thinking. Just do what you'd normally do, except for the over thinking part. Take a shower. Take a shower. Take. A. Shower.

I took a shower. Singing a song to myself. Debating whether I should masturbate before I went see Sasha or not. I was singing a song I made up, about being the last man in the world. I was hard, and shaking my hips to make my dick slap back and forth on my thighs as sort of a drum flourish after each verse. "I'm the last, last man in the world" (flap, flap, flap) "looking, looking for the perfect girl" (flap, flap, flap).

It was maybe because of this I didn't hear the knocking or the busting down of the door or see the shadow falling across the shower curtain until the shower curtain was pulled back and I was screaming and shuddering. Hard-on gone.

Two women in marine fatigues with close cropped hair stood with me in the bathroom. A third woman entered, holding a towel for me, and said don't be alarmed. As I reached for the towel the marines grabbed me and the third woman grabbed my genitals, examined them. She nodded to the other two. "He's the real deal."

"I'm sorry," she explained. "We've had some false reports that ended up being women who underwent sex change therapy." I dried myself with the towel. She said, "Get dressed."

They were very polite and said there had been a citizen's report of a man that was still alive. It was their job to check it out. The sprayed me down with chemicals and then put me in a hazmat suit. I was only thinking how this might mess up my meeting with Amber. It wasn't until well into the ride in the S-

TRAV (Sanitized Transport Vehicle) to the helicopter pad that I realized Amber must have been the one that had reported me. That bitch. She must have talked with her mom about me, who probably said she had a responsibility to report me. That whole thing about her coming down tomorrow with her sister had been bullshit. Maybe the authorities had told her to say that to keep me from leaving my apartment. Or maybe I was being paranoid. Maybe someone just spotted me at the apartment complex peeking out the window.

"Who reported me?" I asked. But the marines just demurred and offered me snacks.

Which I ate.

After touching down in DC, I was whisked to a hospital. Everything was closed off and doors were being opened for me. I was taken to a room and told to sit on a cot. There was an observation window. There were some more women there. It took me a moment to realize the one in the middle was the president.

"Hello, Clay!" she said. I told her hello back.

"You're a very special man, Clay," she said.

"Thank you."

"How does it feel to be the last man on earth?" she asked.

I beamed back. "Pretty good."

"We're going to take some samples if you don't mind. We believe you have some immunity we can use, Clay."

"Okay."

"Is there anything we can get you? A favorite food perhaps?"

"I'd like to see some of my friends. Amber. Sasha. I can give you a list."

The president gave me a thumbs up. "Of course. Give us your list. You'll be meeting a lot of people, if you're okay with that. You're about to be the most famous person on earth," said the president. "Now, if you'll excuse me. God bless you, Clay, and God bless America."

That night I feasted on tacos, pizza, salad, roast beef. (Sushi wasn't available yet. The supply lines were still adjusting.) I got to know my guards and the scientists who were assigned to figuring me out. There was Dr. Monica and Dr. Beth, both thoroughly unattractive older women, but very nice. There was also Veronica, a hot nurse. She had long black hair, just like the girl in the Archie comics. And there were the two marine girls. Adorable. They must have been barely twenty-one. They all laughed at my stupid jokes, were flirty, were happy to talk when I asked them how they were doing, where they were from, their favorite movies, what life was like on the outside now, were there restaurants, was there TV. And I gave them my list of girls I wanted to see, debating whether to add a few movie stars, supermodels, figuring they would be curious enough to come. Hell, they would probably be brought to me, anyway. The president said I was going to meet a lot of people.

I gave them blood. I gave them saliva. Skin swabs. Piss. Hair samples. Semen. A lot of semen.

That night, I lay awake dreaming of being on a regimen of having sex with three different women a day. Young, beautiful women selected for their fertility and genetic diversity. It seemed some rich and powerful women who were maybe not super attractive would want to have sex with me, too. I guess I would be okay with that.

I also fantasized of becoming a movie star, playing all the male roles. I would be lauded for my versatility, adding facial hair or a limp to help differentiate my role as a bad guy from that of the hero. There would be much talk about my nude scenes.

I dreamed of being the head of a parade. Ticker tape coming down. The human race, saved! Hordes of women on either side of the parade yelling, in a twist on Mardis Gras, "Show us your dick!" and me obliging good naturedly to hoots and hollers. It was like being prom king and Superman rolled into one.

I imagined maybe the girls in one of my favorite bands, CAITLIN CAITLIN GLORY HOLE, maybe them all having sex with me. Us hanging out in the studio. Maybe I would do an album with them, a theme album about being the last man. I would write lyrics about how there's a lonely side to being the last man and all women would find me very deep and poignant. The world would agree that they are lucky to have me as their last man. It could have been so much worse.

I felt too alive to be cooped up in my little room. I wanted to ask one of the guards in to sleep with me but I knew that would be against orders. I had to play this cool, not too pervy. I also was prohibited from masturbating except when they wanted me to, because they collected the samples. It was a long several days.

More days passed and when I asked what was going on and I was told to just give it a few more days. Something big was coming, Dr. Beth said.

Then it did. The president arrived with a large group of advisors and a camera crew. I was going to be interviewed on a morning show. They were announcing that they had isolated the disease and yes, I was immune. I would live. My sons would live.

I got dressed and a stylist fussed with my hair a bit and then the host came in. It was Sandra from The Morning Show with Sandra and Pamar. "Our next guest needs no introduction. He is … he is the last 'he' on the planet, it is believed. He's the last man on Earth, Clay Fadiman."

The tone was surprisingly light and breezy. I was asked about my likes and dislikes. My hobbies. What I did for a living back before the plague. My favorite ice cream. A joke about how I felt about the male/female ratio. I played it patriotic. I said I was sad about all the tragedy, but happy that I could do my part to help.

There were more interviews, and then it tapered off. Still I wasn't allowed to leave my lab. I came to think of it as a cell. I was told it took a while for visitors to be cleared. There were risks. Terrorist groups, end of the worlders, people who wanted to finish the job that the plague had started. Although my blood was being shared with scientists throughout the world, there were forces that might try to kidnap me, or kill me, or sell me.

China claimed to have a living man as well, but our government suspected this was a lie to save face.

I said I needed them to give me a date on which I would start getting visits. They kept saying soon.

To placate me, they brought me a computer, books, video games. To my annoyance, the computer had e-mail disabled.

On the Internet I googled my name. There was a band that named themselves after me—The Clay Fadimans. On the website, they all had wigs sort of like my hair and wore shirts like mine and had fake pot bellies.

There were funny videos. One had forty million hits. There was a clip from a live show. A woman was dressed up and imitating the president in a mock up of the Oval Office. Then a chubby little woman came out. In a nasally, nerdy voice she said, "The world needs my semen." I realized this woman was doing a parody of me. Some phrase from my interview had become a catch phrase. Some awkward, idiosyncratic, cringe-inducing way I had said, "The world needs my semen." I didn't even remember saying it, but I had. There were videos that used that sound bite to make a song. It had taken on a life, had become a signifier of what I was.

The funny video continued. The president was seducing me, but first she asked me to put on a mask. The mask was of a prominent movie star, now dead. Dillon Hallow. A mask over my face. The audience laughter swelled and the actors had to pause, waiting for it to die down.

I saw someone had rushed out a book about me. With lots of photos and interviews. And there was Amber talking about me. And Becca, my girlfriend in high school. I was famous, but in the wrong way. Another website sold T-shirts with pictures of me that said: "Not if he's the last man on earth. LOL."

I had to stop watching it all, but I couldn't. I read on. Some scientists were saying one man couldn't provide enough genetic diversity to repopulate the earth anyway. The human race was doomed still and to say otherwise was a lie.

There was a large religion formed in the wake of this catastrophe that worshipped the sacrifice the male gender went through. Their symbol was my face with a line through it. There were photos of it atop steeples, on buildings. I couldn't tell if these photos were faked, as a joke, or if they were real.

It was like all the emotional trauma, all the billions of deaths, all the fathers, brothers, husbands, sons ... all this repressed horror had to be released cathartically. And now that the worst was over, now that a cure had been found, the trauma could come out now. In laughter. At my expense. Almost like it was my fault every other man died. Almost like there was a worldwide wish wondering why couldn't the last man have been someone else. Anyone else.

I told my captors (that is what I came to call them) that I needed a date when I could have visitors, and when I could walk out into the world.

I told them, "No more blood or semen for you until you let me go out in the world." I said I had my rights. I gave them a list of people I wanted to see. Amber. Sasha. A super model. A rock star. A famous actress. "If you don't get me this I will stop eating. I will kill myself. I am an American. I am the last fucking man on earth. I have what you need."

They conferred. And promises were made.

The next day, Dr. Beth came into my room. "We have the band CAITLIN CAITLIN GLORY HOLE here to see you." I jumped up. Yes! "Also, we have Amber scheduled to visit this afternoon. We are just scanning them all right now to make sure they are unarmed."

The marines ushered me to a hallway. I was jittery despite myself. I was starstruck, I admit it. I had to remind myself that technically, I am way more famous than they are. I am the most famous human being on the planet. It was while having thoughts like these that the syringe pierced my neck.

I woke up on a gurney. My arms and legs were strapped down. Around me hung a forest of tubes going off to machines unseen. I looked down with horror to see my abdomen and genitals were opened up, and pierced by a spaghetti of tubes. Tubes in the veins in my legs, tubes in glands, in my kidneys, in my balls. I screamed, and it hurt. I fought against my straps, causing the tubes to flail about.

The doctors and marines rushed in. "I thought you said he was sedated," Dr. Beth snapped. They waited until my screams died down.

Finally, Dr. Beth spoke.

"I'm sorry," she said. "We need to extract your genetic material as quickly and efficiently as possible. I know it sucks, but it is for the good of the world."

"Where are Caitlin Caitlin Glory Hole?" I asked.

The doctors and advisors looked at each other.

"We need to tell him," one said.

"It will just make it worse," said another.

"Tell me what?"

Dr. Beth sighed.

"I can't live like this," I said. "You can't do this to me."

"We can, and we will, because we must," Dr. Beth said. "Executive order. We can never let you outside, we can never risk it. You understand. This is for the good of human kind. I can assure you, you will feel no pain. You will be kept in a permanent coma while we harvest your semen."

I screamed.

"You are a hero."

I screamed until I was hoarse. Then as the meds kicked in things felt okay. I decided it wasn't a big deal. And I drifted off into a white haze, watching the tubes around me fade to white.

7.

That's not really closer to real life.

I thought you just wanted one with Amber in it. This is just one I picked out of a hat.

So everyone in the world hates you. Every woman in the world. Does that seem realistic to you?

Well, not literally every woman. But I guess the ones I was in contact with. Except my mom, of course. And it's not hate, per se. It's just … disappointment? That every other man died but I lived? Who knows what would happen really?

So how do these daydreams make you feel?

I don't know. I don't know what I feel. I'm too busy thinking about the ramifications of the story. I'm too busy thinking to feel.

And what do you feel when it's over? When you've completed one of your stories?

Some degree of satisfaction that it is what would really happen? And some degree of sadness. Maybe.

I want you to use these fantasies to make yourself feel happier, more confident. I want you to have a sexual fantasy where you are amazing. I want—a daydream with a happy ending.

Can I use magic, like a magic potion or something?

Not ideal but I will allow it. The only thing I ask is that in this fantasy, you are desirable. You are a person worthy of love.

Okay. I'll try.

8.

While browsing a weird little shop in Chinatown, I find a little sign that says Love Potions. I inquire about it, and the old woman produces a little bottle. She says if I drink it, women will fall in love with me. The only thing is, I can't drink it in the store, because if I do, she, the proprietor of the store, will fall in love with me. She learned this the hard way when she sold some to a man long ago. Now he is her husband. She laughs.

So I buy some (it's surprisingly cheap) and I take it outside and guzzle it down. It tastes like heartburn medicine, which it probably is, a thick, chalky, mint concoction. With a few drops left, I put a bit behind my ears. I pour a bit in my underwear. I hope this isn't some insecticide. And I think, "Why is your mind letting itself buy into this shit? Even for a second? This sort of stuff isn't real. It's designed to give unhappy people a brief delusional glimmer of hope while separating them from their money."

I drive over to a restaurant where I know a lot of hot people hang out. Hot waitresses, too. I take a seat at the bar and, per usual, the harried bartenders seem to treat me like I'm invisible. People come up to the bar after me and the bartender asks what they want. Still I can't get anyone's attention. All I want is a beer, something to hold, a sort of prop so I don't feel so naked and alone at the bar there as I come to realize what I already know—that love potions are bunk.

Then something happens. One of the girls behind the bar looks at me, really looks at me, and smiles, showing off a dimple on her left cheek. "What can I getcha?" she asks and I swear it's like she's flirting.

I order a Fat Tire. "Good choice," she says. Which it really isn't. She's just saying nice, meaningless things to me. Which is what I do when I like someone. I'm just not used to it being directed at me. Life is so much easier when people just like you. You don't have to be perfect, or brilliant. You can just be yourself.

It's so much easier.

One of the girls standing next to me, she's in a pink neon dress, and with her boyfriend, no less, looks over and notes she likes that brand of beer as well. The boyfriend agrees. Then, get this, pink neon asks me where I'm from. Me! Where I'm from! And I say from around here. I ask where she's from. She says she's from Oklahoma. I say when I get my beer we will toast Oklahoma. And pink neon and her boyfriend laugh like I told a really funny joke. Which I didn't. And I'm happy.

Pink Neon is still looking at me. I look away before she does. She scoots around her boyfriend to be closer to me. Then the cute bartender leans in and hands me my beer. "One beer for toasting Oklahoma," she says. She leans in. She's looking at me, I'm looking at her. It's nice to just look at a pretty girl's face and not have to be secretive or casual or quick about it. The eyes. The nose, mouth, all of it. The little details. Just look at the pretty nose for a bit and not be leering or stealing a glance this time. And I smile and that makes her smile a bit more and that makes me smile a bit more and it's like this chain reaction of happiness. And this must be what it is like to be good looking, or charming, or rich. Suddenly human interaction is very easy. Which is how it should be.

I always thought finding someone who liked you was hard. Hard unless you were beautiful, maybe. But hard for the average people. But I was wrong. It is easy for the average people, too. It's just that I am way, way, below average. Nobody thinks they're below average. Unless it's something factual. Like if you're a dwarf, you have to accept you're below average height. But I guess I had convinced myself I was in the lower middle range of personality and looks. I was not like those people, those perma single people, the really awkward freaky people. Those people who seem asexual. The ones who you wonder what they do at night in their apartments. People that take their hobbies far too seriously. And volunteer a lot at places where they are still barely tolerated, even though they are volunteering their time, for free, for a good cause. People with lots of pets. I thought no, that isn't me. But at some point in life I guess I secretly realized I was. Until this moment.

Pink neon leans in and kisses me. It's like even her eyes were smiling at me. It is the sweetest thing I've ever felt. My eyes are closed and then I feel someone kissing my cheek. The hot bartender? And I feel breasts press up behind me. A hand grabs my shoulder and caresses it. I open my eyes a second to see the cheek kisser is Pink Neon's boyfriend.

I pull back and say "Hey, man," because I'm a quick thinker that way. The girl I was kissing grabs my head roughly and puts her tongue back in my mouth. And the bartender presses her tongue in my ear.

Then another set of hands is grabbing my head and pulling it another way, and the first girl is fighting it. It starts to feel wrong. All of this is going a little far and a little fast and my pants are being pulled down. I want to push the girl kissing me away so I can see who is doing this. There are hands on my legs. My shirt is ripped. Men and women are pressing on me from all directions, climbing on top over the bar. I think I hear a fight breaking out. I'm falling and there's a foot on my calf. Someone else, several people, are sucking my toes.

At this point I remember what that old woman was saying. I was only supposed to use a capful of the stuff. Not the whole bottle. I didn't know what she was saying, her English wasn't good, but I realize now she was emphasizing "Cap full."

I push out and force a pocket of space and try to crawl to the door. The hands clutch harder. A girl is on my back, biting my ear, hard, and I put my fingers into her arm and scratch to get her off. I make a decision and put a sharp elbow at some unseen pillowy mass on me from behind.

I try to slide through the crowd but I'm overpowered. I can't see. I can't breathe. I feel a face and scratch its eyes. It sucks my fingers.

They're ripping my underwear. Hands are fighting around

my dick.

And it's really hot, like a fantasy, but then it's not. They're tearing at my face. They're ripping skin. Pulling off my genitals. They get my stomach open and it's a real free for all. And it hurts so much but it's kind of flattering, too, and I try to feel the sensualness of it behind the pain, but I don't really live long enough to enjoy it. My final vision is a redheaded girl that looks sort of like Amber, like her taller cousin, and she has my intestines and is flossing her vagina with them, getting blood all over her jeans. And in spite of myself I'm kind of flattered she's climaxing with *my* intestines.

9.

Okay. Good first step. Now I want you to have the same fantasy, but you just take a capful.

But I'm dead. I died. I didn't survive getting ripped open.

I know that. But I want you to restart the fantasy.

I tried. But for some reason it goes off the rails. My brain won't let me—

Just try it. I'll see you next week.

10.

While browsing a weird little shop in Chinatown I find a little sign that says Love Potions. I inquire about it, and the old woman produces a little bottle. She says if I drink it, women will fall in love with me. The only thing is, I can't drink it in the store, because if I do, she, the proprietor of the store, will fall in love with me. She learned this the hard way when she sold some to a man long ago. Now he is her husband. She laughs. Also, she cautions me, "Only a capful."

So I buy some with plans to take it when I arrive in Melbourne, Australia. I am going there on business. A convention about medical databases. Or about databases in general. It is not important.

I board the plane just as they're about to close the door. They've already boarded the people on standby and my seat is the last one left. The stewardess informs me, as I try to catch my breath and become aware that my hair is matted in sweat, that I'll need to check my carry-on because all the overhead compartments are full. I fish around for the potion and put it in my pocket, and give the carry-on to the stewardess.

I lurch down the aisle of the plane, my shirt sticky with sweat. I'm looking down and avoiding eye contact for fear of people blaming me for any flight delay. I look around for my seat, a middle one, hoping that my seatmates are attractive women, or, barring that, very small.

It is then I become aware that my seat mates are absurdly hot, ridiculously so. Early twenties, ponytailed, athletic, bright eyed and easy smiled. The one in the aisle seat scoots her knees sideways to let me in. As I scoot by I'm horribly self-conscious about my fat sweaty ass suspended in her face and try to make it all go by quickly and smoothly. I sit, fumbling for my seatbelt, and I graze the girl in the window seat's warm thigh. They help me find the straps, good naturedly lying that the seatbelts can be hard to find sometimes. I finally get situated and feel a tad of relief, despite the shortness of breath, the front seat in my knees, belt cutting in my gut, arm rests cutting into my thighs, and finally look around. My seatmates wear matching T-shirts. Stretched across their breasts a fat cursive logo—50th annual collegiate cheerleading something—distorted by roundness, by wrinkles, always moving from laughter or residual aftershocks from them nodding ascent to a comment made. I can't quite read it all but am afraid to look too long. Some cheerleading event. My cheeks redden. I look around. This whole plane is full of cheerleaders.

After we take off, we are given drinks. The girls have on their headphones. Aisle gets up and goes to the bathroom. When she returns, I ask, "Are you guys going to or coming from?" It comes out like I've forgotten how to talk.

"Going," she says. "Coming back we'll be a lot drunker and have a trophy!"

I'm about to say good luck when the explosion knocks my head into Window Seat's shoulders, and Aisle's head slams into the folds of my torso.

That's my last memory until I wake up.

I'm on my back on the shore of the island. Snot smelling of sea salt. Clothes ripped. Big cut on my calf. Out on the horizon, the last bit of plane sinking. And on the shore, dozens of cheerleaders unconscious, recovering, screaming, foraging, bewildered.

The pilot dies the first night so it is just me and the cheerleaders. Thirty-seven of them. Their clothes are ripped in sort of a sexy post-apocalyptic way. As a morale thing they do some cheers. They form a pyramid. They even include me, I get to hold Jen #1's foot and catch Christy when she spins down. It feels so good to hold her in my arms.

These women are no pushovers. They are can do people. Very quickly leadership roles and committees are formed. Britney #3, exuding a natural confidence and experience as a squad leader, becomes the de facto head. She's tall, willowy, flat chested, manic. She holds her attractiveness in her enthusiasm, her bright smile, her bounding energy, her optimism, her easy laugh. I am in love. I am in love with all of them. I, as the one male on the island, am her de facto co-leader. We set to work tending the wounded, securing a perimeter, hunting for supplies in the wreckage—food, bandages, blankets, luggage with its potluck of contents.

I remember my love potion but it is not in my pocket. It's probably at the bottom of the sea, causing a lucky lobster to suddenly acquire a harem of starfish.

We start a fire so the planes can find us. We find a flare gun with one charge that we keep by the fire. I organize a team to maintain the fire and watch for planes around the clock for the following days, weeks, and yes, months that follow.

I find matches and a pocket knife in a dead man's pants and prove handy with cutting bamboo into makeshift lean-tos. We make small lean-tos that house three girls each. Night falls and we've made lean-tos for everyone except myself. I just say I will sleep outside that night. It is a nice night. Perhaps all the exercise that day has gotten my adrenaline going and given my words an unusual force and confidence, so I am taken at my word. But then when it starts to rain, Britney #3 invites me in. She's in the lean-to with a brunette from the U-Mich squad, Dee.

It's quiet save for the insects, the fire, and the murmurs of cheerleaders up and down the beach. We talk of our families, if they think we're dead, of being on the news, of planes searching for us, of which photos they use of us in the news stories. Lying beside Britney #3, that skinny arm next to me, I can't stop watching the silhouette of her perfect profile as she talks and talks. She says her uncle is in the State House of Representatives in Florida and thus has pull. I lean in to kiss her.

"What are you doing?" she asks, bewildered, sitting up.

"What is it?" asks Dee.

I am prepared for this, and have what I believe is a plausible story. It's probably even true. I say I'm just stressed. I'm scared. I haven't slept in forty-eight hours, and I'm not thinking. I'm sorry.

Britney and Dee excuse themselves to go squeeze in another lean-to. They say it makes sense for me to have my own. I apologize again, and promise I won't try to kiss them and really just want to go to sleep, but soon they're gone.

The next day, as word spreads, I start to be subtly shunned. I am no longer the de facto second-in-command.

I find myself shut out more frequently. Circles of them sitting don't open up quite as much for me anymore. It may be my imagination but the lean-tos around me seem to have moved farther from me over the night. It's a herd mentality. Once I've been rejected by Britney #3, none of the other ones can hook up with me because it makes them seem lower status than her. I feel a shame at blowing this again, and a need to reset the perception of me. Like I need to kill a boar. Or catch a fish.

I do long shifts alone by the fire. Despite being on an island of cheerleaders, I find myself wishing for rescue.

To be honest, although it sounds like a sex fantasy on paper, it really isn't. We're all really hungry and light headed. There's something in the water that makes us all shit constantly. I shit even though I'm not eating enough. Dehydration is a real concern. I'm losing weight but not in a healthy looking way. Lately my thoughts turn to killing one of the cheerleaders for food. Especially that bitch Roni, who especially treats me like shit even though I didn't do a damn thing to her. She's all acting like I'm some creep caught sneaking into the girl's shower when I'm just a castaway like them looking to be around my fellow humans. I'm just standing there trying to catch fish and she acts like I'm ogling her ass or something and does this little "tnnuh" snort. It's always this "tnnuh" with her. Everything I do gives her mild distress. Fuck her. Fuck 'em all. I'll just go to the other side of the island. I'll build a lean-to there. I'll kill tens of wild boars and eat like a king and let them come begging to me. If they are attracted to alpha males, to douchebags, I'll be the biggest douchiest alpha male they've seen. I'll just come to their encampment in the night raping and pillaging. I'll build a fucking crossbow, if I can find some stretchy vines. No, I'll use animal parts. I'll take them all in the night on my enormous member! Impale them like a cheerleader-kabob on my cock!

But of course the reality is far from it. I'm weak from dehydration and not sure if I can even get erections any more. What's more, something, insects or the diarrhea or something, has given me a rash down my ass and thighs and all up my crotch. It looks like I scrubbed my crotch with a cheese grater

136

and sprinkled sawdust or parmesan cheese on it. I have to walk with my legs far apart to keep my thighs from rubbing.

These thoughts, along with leaves and some bird feathers, are my blanket on the cold nights on my side of the island. By then I'm too weak to walk or do much of anything. My guts are on fire. I'm so hungry I've been eating washed up seaweed and drinking salt water. I assume if the girls had been rescued they would have gotten me then. They wouldn't be that dicky, I don't think. But by then I slip into a coma and die and can't really worry about that stuff anymore.

11.

You didn't try.

I did try. I did. I just—my brain isn't under my control. I need help. That's why I come here. For you to help me.

Alright. We need to attack this from a new dimension. I want you to wear a rubber band on your wrist.

Okay.

When you start to have one of these negative fantasies, flick the rubber band. Then refocus your attention to something real. In the here and now. Look at a coffee mug. Look at the clouds. But focus on what is real.

Okay.

That's not all. I also want you to ask out Amber.

Seriously?

12.

I'm in this boring status meeting. We have it every week. The most boring fucking meeting in the world. And it makes me wish I was a peasant in Medieval Europe, or a prisoner, or anything, anything but this death by dullness. And I'm just there zoning out on Amber (she's wearing this flowery layered thing, and tapping her pen on her lip, and I keep wishing I was the pen, on her lip, and then I start to imagine I am the pen, but then I remember to flick the rubber band on my wrist and I focus on the here and now of Tim talking about the status and Amber and the flowery layers and the faux Cherry grain laminate on our conference table.

Then I hear it, the sound of smashed drywall. I look up to see the far wall caving in. A piece of rebar hits Tim on the head. The dust clears and we see that it's not some wrecking ball or a car that ran into the building. Instead, a weird interdimensional portal has opened up. There's these three aliens there with bubbly looking weapons—like pink hair dryers, but ... bubbly. Three really hot aliens, with green skin, and dark green hair, antennae, and each with three huge green breasts barely contained in like these platinum bikinis. And the middle one looks at me and says "You! You are the hero. The prophecy says you are destined to save our people from annihilation ..." And all my coworkers are staring at me as I get up. And maybe I make Amber a little wet. And there's a split second of everyone wondering if I'm going to heed the call to help this planet of three breasted green women, and risk it all and leave my old life behind, or if I am going to say no, no, I'll keep my life on earth thank you, go away. But of course I don't do that.

So then they give me this big parade on this planet full of three breasted green women but it is interrupted by the alien invasion. The invaders look like mean lobsters. They have these angular ships that are just dropping bombs on the cities and on the three breasted green women. Quickly, I'm rushed to the cockpit of this secret weapon they have, this secret spaceship. And there's a plaque that reads GREY FADIMAN, HERO. And I'm not sure why they call me Grey, instead of Clay, but oh well. I take the controls in my hands to fulfill my destiny.

The ensuing battle is short and merciless. I totally fuck up and lose and am enslaved by the lobster guys. They're just roaming around burning the green women and there's nothing to stop them. Finally I put two and two together and realize they had gotten the wrong guy. They thought I was Grey Fadiman. It wasn't really my fault but still I became a pariah in the space league, and am shunned, because here was this amazing species of green women with three breasts and they died on my watch.

13.

So. How did the rubber band go?

Okay, I guess.

Did you fantasize less?

I don't know. Maybe.

And, did you ask out Amber?

I did.

How did it go?

She didn't really answer. She just sort of laughed like I was kidding, but not in a mean way.

Did you ask her what days are good for her?

No.

So what happened then?

I laughed with her like it was all a joke and walked away.

You need to ask her out for real this time. You need to follow through.

Come on. I know I have quote low self-esteem unquote. But I know when people are asked to coffee by people they like, they say yes, cool, and they don't laugh like you're kidding, even though it isn't in a mean way.

Have you thought about seeing a doctor? That might help give you a boost.

You're a doctor. That's ostensibly why I'm seeing you.

I mean a surgeon.

For what?

To remove the growths.

Growths?

Yes.

What are you talking about?

Clay ...

What are you talking about? Where?

Are you suggesting you are in denial about the growths?

14.

I've always had weird theories on why things are like this. Like maybe this is hell. This is my afterlife. Or, I'm in a virtual reality and there's a glitch in the system where all the sex parts of the program got erased. Maybe in a past life I was a sex offender so I was put in this asexual life as karma. Or, here's a theory, maybe just through a combination of genetics and upbringing I'm a basically unappealing person incapable of attracting suitable mates, and the combination of genetics/environment and ignorance/sheer depression keeps me unmotivated and unable to fix it. Maybe it's just that. But I want it to be something else.

But I think, there are people starving and dying, so what the hell is my problem? And maybe I should go help those people. Maybe making other people feel better will make me feel better. Although that's not my main reason for going. Maybe it is. But I bought two tickets to Africa.

Two?

I thought you could go with me, Dr. Ash. If you want.

Oh, Clay. I can't do that.

I know! That is the expected response. But I'm in a rut I can't escape. So why not do the unexpected with me? Let's go to Africa!

Clay …

Either way, I'm going to go. I'm going to stop seeing you. I need to make a change.

I understand. You spoke of theories. I know you've said you wanted me to talk more, respond more to what you have said. Can I tell you my theory?

Of course.

I will have to speak quickly, because we don't have much time.

It's the beginning of the session.

That's not what I mean. You'll understand.

Okay.

Are you ready? Are you ready for my theory?

Yes.

This universe has 173 dimensions.

I see.

Let me finish—

Is this some new age stuff? Are you going to sell me some crystals?

The world has 173 dimensions. Most creatures can sense all the dimensions, and live in all of them. But some creatures have defects that make them unable to perceive the other dimensions, so they are "blind" to all but fifty dimensions, or twenty-five, or, in your case, four.

Me? Me specifically? Or me in the general sense of human kind me?

You specifically. It's hard to explain and I have to speak clearly before they get here.

Who?

I don't have time. So, there are parts of you in all the dimensions, and they are linked. But you just can't sense it, like a leg that has no feeling. It's still there. For example, let me see. For example, in dimensions seventeen through twenty-six you are linked psychologically with a swarm of bat/spider like creatures. Have you ever sometimes felt your mood suddenly get happy and a bit manic for no apparent reason? It happens when these bat creatures attack their prey, you will get those feelings. Those bat creatures are a part of you, and you are linked.

And here's the deal. Your balls, your vas deferens, in this dimension, they are linked to a heart bomb testicle planet in dimension 173—well, not really a heart bomb testicle planet, it's hard to explain seeing as you are dimensionally blind.

But the point is, if you were ever to ejaculate in this dimension, the heart bomb testicle planet will collapse on itself and the whole universe collapses on itself. All 173 dimensions, the end of everything. At least that's the theory.

You're mocking me.

I'm not. You have to believe me.

I get it. You're mocking my fantasies so I realize the stupidity of them. But your theory doesn't stand up to logic. I *have* ejaculated. Plenty of times. Some of those times have even been inside women. And the world has not ended.

You just think you have. It's implanted memories, like you said.

You're onto it more than you realize. And you <u>are</u> always at work, except when you are in these sessions. Your feeling is absolutely correct.

Every evening as work is about to end we pick you up and plop you back at the beginning of your day in the time intersections. It's like —like putting a rat back in the beginning of the maze.

That logic doesn't hold up. Why don't you just kill me? If I'm that much of a risk?

My government believes killing is a sin. We can't do it. Plus, our scientists fear that your death might also set off the end of the world. So we have to keep you on this permanent loop. It's not easy.

Are there other people like me?

No, just you. Your feelings of childish narcissism are in fact warranted. Thank God it is just you. You don't realize how difficult it is, maintaining this charade. There's a government agency devoted to it. It's seven percent of the budget. Making sure you don't get laid, that you stay in this loop. Maintaining your presences in the other dimensions, and keeping the signal scrambled so you can never sense yourself in the other dimensions.

Then why even let me see a shrink?

Don't you get it? I'm not helping you at all. My advice is terrible, designed to keep you in the dark. Telling you to try to control your fantasies more, when we control them. Or telling you to ask out Amber—she's one of ours. She will only deflate your ego more.

Why are you telling me this now?

There are those that believe your heart bomb testicle planet will not destroy the universe. There are those that believe that you are kept alive not getting laid merely so people can keep their jobs. There's a lot of money involved, manipulating these dimensions. Preventing saboteurs.

There are those that believe that maybe the heart bomb testicle planet should go off. Maybe it will make the universe better and usher in a new utopia. Or, if it ends the universe, maybe that is the natural order of things and it will be reborn.

I am part of this resistance. Many have died so that I could get this close to you. I had hoped to make you more ready, but they're on to us. We are running out of time. You will never go to Africa, Clay. You will have no memory of this conversation. They will kill me. You will have a new shrink, and a strange feeling that something isn't quite right.

What can I do?

You must ejaculate now. With me. Are you willing to do it? Are you willing to risk it?

I am.

She stands up, removing her blouse. Her breasts spill out. She grabs for my belt buckle. I get a weird feeling. A feeling of confidence and elation.

Right now, the resistance is coming to you in all different dimensions. Our fleet is landing on your heart bomb testicle planet, to caress it. In another place, you are a duck, in another a dwarf and we arranging for you to meet a princess. You are a cube of energy in a cage of sparks and also a skeletal host. It is hard to explain. Timing is critical. Do you want to enter me? Or jerk off on my tits? Forgive me, let me handle it. I've been trained. There's just no time! It wasn't supposed to be like this. Also, you must realize, we won't be having conventional four dimensional sex. It's going to get … weird. Just keep looking in my eyes. Keep your tongue in my mouth and let me do the rest.

I nod. She takes my penis and puts it in her. The walls of the doctor's room fall away and we are falling in pure sky. Her books are falling everywhere and turning into birds.

I have wings. I am a hang glider. I look up and on the moon is Dr. Ash's face. *Fly towards me,* she says. I look down. I am hard, and Dr. Ash is hanging on my dick like it's a handle and she's a subway commuter.

I reach the moon and am inside it. The moon is her body, but her body is facing me. She has somehow turned inside out and I am inside her and she is facing me from all around. Rips start to occur in her in perfect face. "That's the government agents cutting through my defenses. Please, you must come. Look at my breasts."

She continues to stroke my penis in several dimensions and the elation continues. I can only feel it vaguely, but I feel tremors of things that are happening to me in other places, like forgotten muscles, or things in other worlds. There's a feeling in me, like a planet, a planet of hot molten lead starting to rumble.

She moans. I moan. Our eyes fill with light.

See you on the other side. If this works.

And then it explodes. Not me. The moon with Dr. Ash's head explodes and a starship is flying towards me. It is close but feels so far away. It fires a fusillade of something that stings like ice. The heat grows but distant feelings shift to wrongness—to fear—like something is draining my energy cube, firing shotguns

146

at my inter-dimensional duck self, hatcheting my dwarf, howling jets dropping emergency sheets of ice down over the heart bomb testicle planet.

Dr. Ash's leg moves up through a cloud, her giant leg, to swat the starships, and her shoe flies off and explodes. They take evasive action. I feel like I'm falling again, through clouds, through rug burns, through a salty taste, through fire. But still it feels good and Dr. Ash is with me. It feels so good I don't want to release it. But it can't be stopped. I hope it won't be stopped.

Don't hold it in, she says. *Go, go, go.*

Dr. Ash squeezes me from all directions as the starships bear down for another run. Now I am the planet, and they are flying over my peaks and valleys, firing, firing. *Now,* she says. *Now. Don't look back. Don't think. DO it.* And I wonder if the world will really end, and if so how, and then

1.

"I feel like I'm always at work."

Dr. Lipsyte cleans his pipe. It's amazing to me someone in their early eighties still smokes, I think. I also think, I really need to get a prettier shrink. It's another thing I never seem to get around to. I think I write it on my to-do list but then it's never there. I guess I dream it. But I guess it's unhealthy, wanting a pretty shrink. But Lipsyte. I don't know. He looks at me calmly, with just a hint of … is it contempt? Boredom? Fear?

What do you think about, when you're always at work?

ACKNOWLEDGEMENTS

Many months, maybe years (is it years? Time goes by so fast, doesn't it?) later you're at the grocery store just to get a few quick items—artichokes for a salad, some dental floss. And there at the cash register (to be clear, it's a line of the self-serve registers but there at the head to make sure it all runs smoothly) is, with a little red vest that matches his skin is that little sidekick of the host in that book you read. Snively, or something, or else someone who looks damn near like him. You're a little too unsure to say anything, though.

"Hey!" he says. He recognizes you. He calls you by name. "How's it going? Did you ever finish that book I was in? I never did, because I was a bit pissed I wasn't in all of it. But I should read it. I should. Did you finish it? Was it good?"

"Oh, I loved it," you say, with maybe too exaggerated enthusiasm. In truth you thought there were some good parts, some not so good parts. It was sort of uneven. But there are some bits you still remember, so that's something. "But the parts you were in were the best. It wasn't as good after you left, Snivelly."

"Snervely," he corrects. You wince, but luckily you see the little involuntary increase in his smile, maybe not an increase but a change, subtle, from a customer service-y smile to a genuine smile, so that his lips didn't really change their shape but still it changes somehow, as I said, subtly, shows he's pleased by your flattery.

"Do you still have a copy? I'd love to borrow it some time."

"Absolutely," you say. At this point you break eye contact to get the scanner to read the UPC code for the can of artichoke hearts, but are careful to look back at Snervely fairly soon, so as not to seem rude. You don't offer your contact info or anything, and you hope he doesn't ask. The truth is, you think you still have the book, but you might not. You did a purge some time ago and took a big box of books to Goodwill. You think to point out you're sure he can buy the book used online, for as little as twenty cents or so, but then you think the fact that the book he was in, maybe the only book he'll *ever* be in, is selling so cheaply that his feelings might be hurt so you say nothing and go on to scanning your dental floss.

"Hey," says Snervely. "One other thing. The author would like to thank some people. First off, his earliest readers, main advisors, and good friends: Todd Smarrella, Branden Waugh, and Dave Willis. He'd like to thank his awesomely supportive wife, Heather; his children, Ava and Maggie; his parents, Linda and Larry; and his sister, Amy. He wants his family to know he's saving their well-deserved front page dedication for a book with fewer naughty bits. He'd like to thank Jack Pendarvis, Joe Randazzo, and Charles Yu - three brilliant writers that the author admires who despite being busy, successful people and also perfect strangers were kind enough to read the book and write kind words about it. The author feels getting to know them a bit was one of the most rewarding parts of the endeavor. He'd also like to thank Mykle Hansen for his kindness and editing. He'd like to thank Mike Lazzo and Keith Crofford for many things. He'd like to thank Brendan Mathews, Jessa Marsh, Steve Himmer, Kevin Donihe, Jay Edwards, Max Forstater, and Matt Schwartz for their support in the early self-doubting period (as well as the later self-doubting period) and he'd like to thank still more people, such as especially good English teachers, but feels it is a bit hubristic to thank too many people unless your book is really kick ass. He doesn't think this book is kick ass, maybe he hopes parts of it are, but hell, he got over his fear and did it. It was the best he could do at this moment in time. He finished something he set out to do, which is a good thing to do in life. A good thing to do while we're hurtling to the void, all of us. And most of all he'd like to thank you, specifically, for reading this book. He knows you have a lot of other options. He hopes he made you feel a bit less alone. He knows the thought of you reading this has made him feel a bit less alone."

By now the bag handle is cutting into your hand a bit. Well, maybe that's an exaggeration, it's a very light bag, but you are a bit tired of standing there. But then a question bubbles up.

"Whatever happened to your cohost?" you ask. You would ask about him by name, but you can't remember if it was Badbones or Badbrainz. It was probably Badbones, because Badbrainz was a band, wasn't it?

You're guessing maybe he's become a host again of something else, or maybe he killed himself. But what Snervely tells you is nothing so dramatic. Badbones ended up getting that job at the medical supply place with his brother. And he remarried. And he's gotten into running.

And with that you get your receipt and depart. You wave to Snervely.

"Good-bye!"

EPILOGUE

It was a day like the others—where he could work mostly on automatic. The flat, blank sky outside the window was the perfect empty canvas he once might have used to paint the day's daydreams. Swashbuckling, etc. But he didn't daydream much anymore. It slowed and slowed and then one day it just dried up. The sky became a blanket to wrap the dried up parts, so comfortable they didn't even know they existed anymore.

The worker reached for the stapler and the stapler slid of his reach, like it was pulled on a string.

"Actually," said the stapler, "I was hoping you'd use Jenny for this job."

"Jenny?" said the worker.

"Your coffee mug."

"My coffee's mug's name is Jenny?" The worker looked at the mug, the navy blue mug, with its company logo in gold.

"She's looking to get into stapling. I notice these documents are press clippings. They're not critical. You usually keep them for thirty days out of obligation and then they go to the recycle bin. I think this is a good job for Jenny to test the waters, get her ears wet."

"I'm ready," said the mug.

The worker put the mug down. "But listen," the worker said to the stapler. "You have a specific set of parts designed to hold the staples, push them through the paper, and bend them neatly. The coffee mug has none of these. The coffee mug is shaped perfectly to hold coffee. And see how my hand fits in the handle."

"That's just thinking inside the box," said the stapler, who introduced himself as Terry. "You haven't even tried."

The worker found himself pushing a staple through the papers with the coffee mug. Bending them around. It took a couple of tries. It wasn't perfect.

"But it's a great first run. Look at that," admired the stapler.

The mug beamed, the corporate logo on the side of the mug distorting slightly.

"It's kind of wonky," the worker said.

"But are the papers staying together?"

"Yes," the worker said.

"And isn't that the primary function of stapling?"

"Yes," the worker said, not appreciating the stapler's condescension.

"There you go. And I guess now's as good a time as any to tell you I don't want to be your stapler anymore."

The worker suppressed a laugh. "Do you want to be my coffee mug?"

"No," said the stapler. "I want to be a staple. I've worked with staples, I like them. Many, many staples have gone through me. I like the idea of just sitting on my ass, holding paper together. I want to see how the other half lives."

"Okay," the worker said. "Do you have a preference of what sort of papers you'd like to be stapled in?"

"I'm sorry if I gave you the wrong impression. I don't want to be a staple for you," said the stapler. "I'm doing a little start-up. With Jenny. That's how you get the big bucks."

"I see."

"We're looking for talented self-starters, if you're looking to jump ship. The only thing is, does your name end in Y?"

"My name is Branden," said the worker.

"Could it be Branden-y? Because that way all of our names end in y. And we could be The Y Team."

"I could be Branden-y," said the worker.

"What would you bring to the table?" asked the stapler.

"I procure collection systems," said the worker.

"Not really a need for that. What else you got?"

Out of the worker's mouth, to everyone's surprise including the worker, came, "Swashbuckling."

"Swashbuckling," repeated the stapler, rolling it around a bit in his smallish metal mouth. "Swashbuckling. There's buckles. Lots of buckles. And they're going to need to be swashed. But where do you go for that? Yes. Swashbuckling. I see a real untapped market in that."

The coworkers saw the worker leaving with his coat, his briefcase, his mug, his stapler.

"A little early for lunch," the manager said.

Outside, Branden, Jenny, and Terry got into the wastepaper basket that wanted to be a car and away they went.